LOVE HATES US ALL

LAWRENCE SAVAGE

Ellenese Publishing

Dedicated to the lost souls searching for a home.

The cover drawing is by Rohan Singh Kalsi.

ISBN 978-1-8383774-1-0

An outsider's pursuit for love and happiness in a

hypocritical world.'

-Lawrence Savage

Some days I sit back and
think
If love was ever meant for
me
Because my previous
attempts made me see
I was never the lover I
thought I would be
Had good love
And I made her unhappy
Had bad love
And I made her regret
leaving me
If I loved you once
I'll love you forever
If I lose one
I'll attract another
Does that make me a
heartbreaker or a
womanizer?
Or just someone that
doesn't have his life
together?
Never been the type to
plan

So in some ways I've never
been the ideal man
How can you build a
future with someone
That's stuck in their past
Escaping their reality
By reminiscing about
everything he had
I think I'm a good man
I'm just bad at love
For me love means pain
But then again
Pain and life are
intertwined
And without love there can
be no life
So I'll continue this lonely
pursuit
Until I'm no longer alive
Who knows?
Reading this you might
even agree
That maybe
Love wasn't meant for me

- Charles Johnson

1

Every summer something drastic happens in my life, it's either I fall in love or fall out of love or a mixture of both. I don't know. Maybe it's because I spend most of my time drinking. I like alcohol. Maybe more than I like women, if that's even possible. Alcohol makes the world blurry and my thoughts clear. A writer's strongest weapon is his word, and alcohol made me the deadliest man alive. Drinking gives me a certain confidence that is absent when I'm sober, I can feel it in my writing, in my poetry, in myself. Usually, I would pour myself a glass of whiskey, put on sad songs and sit at my desk. That was my writing process. I would turn down the brightness on my laptop and continue drinking until I was no longer able to see what I was typing. I preferred to let my emotions do the writing instead of logic. I think that's what's wrong with the world today, we put so much emphasis on everything being done with logic and reasoning that we neglect the emotional aspect of it. That's why everything seems so fake nowadays. The people. The world. The women. The love. It's all fake. There's an element of authenticity and rawness that's missing in us and it's all because we fail to embrace our emotions. No one wants to be vulnerable anymore because we are all scared of getting our feelings hurt and our hearts broken. It's ironic. An emotionless world filled with emotional people.

The worst part about having friends that are musicians in the big city is being forced to surround yourself around the fakeness that comes with that lifestyle. Jack invited me to the listening party his label was having for one of their artists. I said yes, not because I was musically curious, but rather out of boredom. It was summer and leaving the house meant having an excuse to drink. So here I was surrounded by deadbeat aspiring artists who felt like the whole world revolved around them and that who you knew, how many followers you had and what you did, determined how much effort they should put into getting to know you. I hated big cities. No matter where in the world you went, they all had the same poisonous mentality. Bunch of judgemental people going broke trying to impress each other in a city that's too busy to care. I've always been an in-between type of man. Not too small, not too big. I preferred that, because at least then you could create the city you wanted. The same way I prefer my women. Not too big, not too small. Not too caring, not too cold. Not too ugly, not too beautiful. Too beautiful scared me, too ugly disgusted me and too much of everything broke me.

Standing there listening to him talk, I kept wondering how someone could live a life that was so out of touch with reality. It's truly amazing the lies we can convince our mind to believe when our heart is our advocate.

'That's why I dropped out of business school man, that's not what I wanted you know. Life is too short to not pursue what you want. That's why I started this label, and so far, it's going well. I've had several meetings with the A&R for both Universal Records and Sony Music and they taught me a lot about the industry. Bro I've been so busy lately setting up concerts, it's crazy'. His name was Alan. He was a university drop out. He knew important people. He was just like everybody else. What is it with people in our generation and the need to showcase our latest achievements whenever someone asks, 'how are you doing?'. This was the second time I met Alan, but the first time we had a full conversation, and I must say he did not disappoint. He lived up to be the big city guy I thought he would be, you know the type that measures their value in life by how important they are in other people's eyes.

'That's good, continue doing what you love.'

'What about you, how is your writing going? Jack tells me your poetry is some of the best he's ever read.'

'Jack is a good friend, but a terrible liar. And I don't know, I haven't done any writing lately.'

'Oh really, why not?'

'Because I've been happy.'

'Oh, okay that's cool. Anyways, it was good talking to you, I always liked your vibe. Do you have social media?'

'No, I don't.'

'So how do you talk to people?'

'I don't.'

Vibe. I hate that word. Slowly but surely, our generation has ruined the English language by using unnecessary words, initialisms and abbreviations as a way to communicate. LOL. LMAO. STFU.

Alan left soon after to entertain other people with his amazing conversational skills, and I made my way towards the end of the rooftop. It was truly a beautiful view I thought as I lit a cigarette. The orange sunset crept behind the skyline of skyscrapers and tall office buildings that crowded the central part of the city. This was the type of view that would make a photographer climax. There's something about sunsets that just makes everything better, it gives the world a beauty that we don't see during the day. No matter how fast paced your life is, your eyes will never fail to notice a beautiful sunset. I checked my phone to see if I had received any notifications. I always had a love and hate relationship with my phone, and since I couldn't get rid of it, I decided to put it on do not disturb mode. I opened up my messages and I saw that I had received a text from Sylvie Bardot. I've wanted to fuck her since I was twelve, I think once upon a time I even loved her too. But mostly wanted to fuck. No matter how hard I tried, it never worked. In the end I decided to settle for friendship, at least that way I could keep her close to me. It was a win for friendship, and a defeat for my cock. Thinking of a response to her text it shocked me that I didn't know. What does one respond when you receive a text saying 'Hey, how are you?'. Do I be honest and tell her that I wake up every day feeling like shit? That I feel like my life no longer has any meaning, and I just spend my time existing rather than living? That I chase away every good love that comes my way because I feel like I don't deserve it? In the end I decided to lie. It was much easier that way. Less emotions, less explanation. Not every woman can handle an emotional man, and not every man can handle a woman. 'Hey, I'm fine. Just in the city attending a listening party. How are you?'. There. Text sent.

Luckily, I didn't have to wait long until I got a call. It was Sylvie.

'Chuck, how long are you staying in Paris for?'

I always liked her voice. It was neither feminine nor masculine; it was just right. High pitched voices put me off, how could someone sound happy all the time? That should be a criminal offence.

'I don't know how long I'm staying for; it all depends on what I end up doing.'

'Ok, come see me. I have an apartment not too far from the botanic garden. I'll text you the address. When can you come?'

'Now.'

I said my goodbyes and left the party. Thank God. I
disliked parties. It was the same thing all over again.
Same people, different faces. Same music, different
artists. I was supposed to take tram number 11 into the
east side of the city, and from there embark on a ten-
minute walk towards Sylvie's apartment. I liked public
transports. In some ways each tram, train or bus ride
was a novel with different characters. Sitting there
trying to imagine what kind of life, story and
background each person had was a great way to make
time pass for a man that hated his phone. However, on
that day I didn't want to think. I was tired of thinking.
Sometimes thinking is the ruination of everything
good.

It was 7.45 pm when I found myself in front of her apartment. It wasn't the easiest to find, considering that in some way, shape or form all apartment complexes in Paris look alike. Big tall brick buildings with signs of construction work being done on them. I guess it wasn't a big city apartment if there were no signs of constant improvement. I rang on apartment 101, heard a buzz and then a click from the door. Sylvie opened the door with a big smile and gave me a hug. Standing there in her black summer dress my eyes kept admiring her body. Either she chose the right dress, or God gave her the right body. Either way she looked stunning with her tan skin tone, green eyes and dark brown straight hair that was curled up at the ends. Her apartment was simple, and yet just enough. Painted in white and spacious, it was the type of minimalistic apartment you would expect in the big city. Her two roommates sat in the living room drinking wine. I walked over, introduced myself and sat down. Their names were Amanda and Helena. Amanda was stocky built, brunette and from the western part of the country, meaning that she had an accent I didn't like. Whiles, Helena was your ideal European woman. Blonde straight hair, blue eyes and skinny, meaning that she wasn't my type. In another universe she would've been a model, well who knows, maybe I'll see her on the front cover of Vogue one day. I like girl talks. Sitting there, drinking wine, talking about love and everything it comes with, the butterflies, the emotions, the breakup, the healing. It might be because I love *love*. And when you love something you want to talk about it, feel it, and even serenade it with poetry. Women dive into the deep end in their conversations about love, whiles us men only dip our feet in. Amanda hated men, Helena loved them, and Sylvie was in-between. In a weird way I agreed with all of them.

'All men are the same. They are all ungrateful and emotionally selfish.'

I liked Amanda; she had a realistic view on love.

I asked her what made all men ungrateful.

'Because you guys don't know how to appreciate a good woman.'

'What is a good woman?'

'A woman that loves you.'

'Okay, then what is a bad woman?'

'A woman that hates you.'

'Has love ever been that simple?'

'Yes, before men decided to complicate it.'

Helena seemed skeptical the whole time whiles Amanda was talking, and I could tell she was dying to stand up for the gender she loved so much.

'I don't know Amanda; I feel like when it comes to men it depends on how much you mean to them. Very often we like to think that we carry more importance in a man's life than we actually do. A man will risk it all and do it all for the right woman.'

In a sense they were both right. Men don't know how to appreciate women until the right one comes along, and even then, we still don't appreciate them enough, but at least we will try to. During the conversation I found myself thinking about Célia, and Amanda was right; us men don't know how to appreciate a good woman. Every woman on earth could have my heart, but only Célia had my soul. Most days we hated each other, some days we loved each other. In the end the shouting got less, and the sex got worse, and she decided to leave. I guess a woman that no longer wants to kill you or fuck you, is a woman that's done with you. And here I was, a man alone in an apartment with three fuckable women thinking about a love long gone. A romantic tragedy in a city filled with misery.

We talked more and drank more, until it was only Sylvie and I left. Sitting on the couch with our bodies facing each other, we started reminiscing about old times, the good and the bad. Mostly the bad.

'I can't believe I ended up moving to the other side of the world for a man that ended up cheating on me. You know Chuck, whenever I think about the situation I just feel like the dumbest woman on earth.'

'You're not dumb, you were just in love. And whenever the heart leads, the mind weakens. Love as an idea is in itself crazy. We are granted one life, and we are supposed to spend every moment of that life with only one person until one of us dies or falls out of love. When you have it, society thinks you're finished, and

19

when you're without it they make you feel like you're incomplete.'

'You always have a way with words, don't you?'

'No, this is just some good ass wine.'

We shared a half laugh as our eyes caught each other. After a brief second of silence, I decided to break it by leaning in to kiss her. She kissed me back as if she planned for this to happen. It's fascinating how a woman will never tell or show you when they want to be kissed, fucked or loved. You just have to hope for the best and prepare for the worst. We went into her bedroom, undressed and laid down in bed. I climbed on top of her, kissing her viciously whiles fondling her breast with my hand. I could feel her nipples harden, and my cock rise. Having her perky shaped breast in my mouth I felt like the most powerful man on earth. The feeling of a man that just accomplished his greatest goal. I put my hand down her panties, carefully rubbing her clit. It was wet. Making my way down her body with my mouth, starting from the neck until I reached her inner thigh, I didn't even get to settle my mouth on her cunt before she started moaning. Either I was an oral God, or she hadn't had sex in while. I chose to think I was the former. I enjoyed pleasing a woman orally, it's the least I could do for her wanting to have sex with me. It's a sad reality that most women don't understand that they have the power when it comes to sex. They can deny it, or they can allow it. The man just has to accept whatever it is. Listening to her moan as she held my head down with her arm, I felt a burning sensation inside of me and yet my cock wasn't rising.

'I don't know what's happening, it won't come up.'

'What are you talking about?'

'My cock, it doesn't want to rise. That goddamn wine.'

We tried everything. Fingering, blow job, hand job, every kind of job. It just wasn't working. I felt a sudden rush of betrayal. My greatest love decided to let me down when it mattered the most. How could you alcohol? I thought we had a great relationship; I gave you my money and you made my pain disappear. I felt like a general that just lost a war. The only thing more painful than defeat is death, and I guess my day hadn't come yet. But this night was close. Spending most of my youth imagining how she looked naked, I now had her in front of me and I couldn't perform. I guess friendship was the only thing we would have besides from a morning of regrets and second thoughts.

'I'm sorry Sylvie, I'm really sorry. I can continue going down on you if you want?'

I had the tone of a salesman that hadn't sold a single car for a whole week, sadness. Utter sadness.

'No, it's fine. Let's just go to sleep.'

As we turned around to go to sleep, I held her close to me and yet we couldn't be more distant. What a sad ending for a sad night in a sad life. I could just imagine her texting her friends after I leave.

CHARLES JOHSON

THE WORST MAN I'VE EVER HAD IN BED

The morning after, she was still looking beautiful and my heart was still shameful. Ironically enough my cock was hard. Was it due to her beauty or my morning routine of being horny? She came back into the room with two glasses of water. Even after a sexless night she still wanted to care of me. Amanda was right, men don't know how to appreciate a good woman. We spoke for a bit before I put my clothes on and left. Sitting on the bus that was taking me to the train station, I kept looking at those around me wondering what they thought of me. I wondered what Sylvie thought of me. In the end I reached the conclusion that they thought the same. Here was a man that couldn't get his life together or his cock up. If a man isn't successful in life or isn't able to please a woman, what then is his worth? I sat there thinking about Célia, everything I had, and everything I had lost, as I asked myself if love hates us all.

2

The illusion of love can seem so real, that we forget that everything in this world is *temporary*. No matter how hard we try our love will die, either by choice or by force. And no matter how much you want to; you can never love someone's sadness away. To some my view on love might seem pessimistic, to others realistic, but in the end it's my reality. I felt hate before I experienced love, which always made me wonder what love was. In some ways I'm very much like my mother, and in other ways like my dad. I share my mother's hatred for this world, and my father's love for women. I liked my mother more. Love is complicated with rules, instructions and labels. Hate is at least direct, honest and won't fuck you over. And yet I always chose love, no matter how many times it cheated on me and broke my heart I always went back. Fool me once shame on you, fool me twice shame on me, fool me three times *okay but don't do it again*.

My father's fondness for women made him afraid of settling down with one and raising a family. My mother left me with my grandparents when I was two years old, so she could move to the United States in her pursuit of a better life. And to be honest I couldn't blame her. Living in Sierra Leone in the nineties, there was nothing the country could offer you aside from civil war, poverty and misery. I visited my mother twice a year, and each time around she would shower me with lavish gifts, designer clothing and the newest technology. Sometimes I wonder if she did it out of love or *guilt*? I never cared for the materialistic stuff and growing up I never cared for her either. Every holiday spent in her house was a constant reminder of how unwanted I was. A father that despised the idea of having me in his life, and a mother that could only stand being with me for a limited time. And after each trip I would sit on the plane back home to a grandfather that made my life a living hell, and a grandmother that tried her best to *accept* me. My search for love as a child always led back to the same questions. Was there something wrong with me? Why did it seem like no one wanted me? Was I a bad child? Watching other families around me, I learned that love comes easy. I was just a hard person to love.

Five years after my mother left, I moved to France with my grandparents. We lived in *Reims*, a city that had the charm of a small town due to its population size and the rough character of a big city. I grew up in Croix Rouge, a part of the city well known for its poverty-stricken neighborhoods and high crime rate.

I hated the city, but I always had great love for my area. The same place that made me tough, was also where I first experienced love. A community brought together through financial hardships, and where no one was better than the other. In some ways we all had experienced pain as we searched for an escape from our sadness through laughter and companionship. I had a close circle of friends I hung out with every day. Stealing from stores, running from police, playing sports, getting into trouble at school. It was fun. Growing up we had everything we needed, we just didn't have *enough*. Each of us had our own problems and were fighting our demons, but in a strange way we never talked about our troubles. We just accepted the fact that that's how life was.

My grandfather was a peculiar man. A mind filled with ambition, goals and dreams stuck in the body of a man that was filled with anger, sadness and lack of resources. He always wanted more, dreamt of more, but there wasn't anything more life could give him aside from a big pile of debt and an underpaid job at a restaurant. Always starting projects that he could never finish, and using more money than he earned, my grandmother had the burden of being the caretaker of the house. Every day coming home from school I was met with a beating, and during every conversation he would break me down little by little until I felt weak and broken. As time went on his relationship with my grandmother grew weaker. They would often argue, ending with her in tears and leaving me to console her.

I still remember the day he called me into his room. 'Charles, you may see your grandmother cry and think that I'm a bad person, but when you get older you will see that I'm not as bad as she paints me out to be.' I never understood what he meant but looking back at it now I think he was right. He was never a bad man; he was just *sad*. Here you had a man whose whole life was filled with regrets, and every attempt to achieve something resulted in failure. He passed away when I was seventeen and left behind a huge debt that my grandmother now became responsible for. I remember standing in front of my best friend Henry at his funeral, embracing him with a hug as I said, 'he's gone' and started crying. I cried because I was no longer suffering under his pain. I cried because I was no longer shackled down by his poisonous chain. I cried because I was tired of screaming after all those times, he left my heart aching. Those were not tears of sorrow, but tears of a man that was finally *free*. Over two hundred people attended his funeral, but as someone that spent my whole life with this man, I could barely recognize those people. It's ironic how people show more love for you when you're dead than they tell you when you're alive. I hated it. I hated the fake love. Sitting at the service and hearing everybody speaking highly of him, I felt angry. None of those people knew the hell he put us through, the financial struggle he brought upon us, and the way he ruined every loving bone I had in me. He made me cold and heartless. Leaving my grandmother to put food on the table and a roof over our heads, I always wondered how he could be happy with himself but finding out after his death that he was an alcoholic, I guess he wasn't. Sometimes when I look at my grandmother, I don't know if she's happy or sad that he's gone. Because looking at their relationship, it must be a weird feeling to love and hate someone at the same time. Wanting to hug and kiss them but also wanting to pack and leave them.

I was diagnosed with adhd when I was seven and depression when I was sixteen. As a child, growing up in a household where I wasn't allowed or given the chance to express my emotions forced me to bottle up my feelings inside. But a human can only go for so long until he or she explodes, and due to my temper, one could say I exploded sooner than others. This led to me getting into trouble at school and finding myself in situations I shouldn't have been in just because I had so much bottled up inside and it seemed like no one cared enough to sit me down and ask me how I was. My elementary school felt that I was too much trouble, so they called in an agency that dealt with difficult children to assess and oversee my development which they conducted by sending a psychologist to my school that sat in the back of the class taking note of every little thing I did and then once a week tried to have a half-ass conversation with me. Imagine a person with a totally different life and childhood than yours telling you how you should feel or act, imagine a person that came from a financially stable and good home with loving parents telling you a struggling child whether or not your life is hard. The fucking audacity. I hated that agency and those people, and whenever they came, I made sure I gave them a worthy show since they had already put a *label* on me as the angry foreign kid. That's the word, label. Before I could even figure out who I was, society had already put a label on me and stamped me out to be something I wasn't. Yes, I got into fights, yes, I could be an inconvenience at times, but no I was never a bad child. I was an immigrant that had moved from his home because of the war and was now placed in an unfamiliar environment where I experienced racism and discrimination on a daily basis, an environment that brought me more pain than growth and more frustration than understanding. My childhood denied me the chance to express myself and my life taught me how to cope with problems on my own since my attempts at opening up and revealing the darkest sides of my mind always lead to me being alone. Most people I've trusted and opened myself up to would tell me how much they understood my pain and that they would never leave me, but when you've been told all these lies throughout your life at a certain point a cold heart will end up replacing the tears in your eyes. Throughout this crazy journey called life, I've found it hard to cope with not only having adhd but also suffering from depression which is why I found relationships so tiresome and draining because a combination like that means that your depressed mind will go in a hyperactive state in which negative and suicidal thoughts will overshadow your mind and slowly but painfully ruin your will to live. During such times you often find it difficult explaining your emotions and sadness to those around you, because how can you open up and let someone into a mind and plethora of thoughts you have no *control* over or understanding of. The resentment of having to answer when people continuously ask you if you're okay leads to a sensation of wanting to escape and be in your own solitude. That lingering wish of wanting to be alone made it hard for me to be in a loving relationship with others, because how could you tell someone you love that you wish you could go weeks without speaking to them, or that you most days don't feel like waking up. Although I'm a caring man this made me feel like I was terrible at love, because how could I love someone else when my mind is clouded with hate, hate towards myself, my life, and this world. It's an excruciating feeling when you know that your partner is deserving of a love you cannot provide for them, not because you don't want to but rather because you can't. How can you love someone else when you're struggling to love yourself? I've spent most of my life surrounded by bad, hurtful, and painful love, that's the only type of love I've come to know, and sometimes I feel like that's the only type of love I deserve. Being with me will include days where you cry, days where you're confused, and days where you feel unloved. I'm not good at love and I'm starting to think that the universe with my previous relationships is showing me that love is not good for me either. I've been in bad relationships in which I was unhappy because I felt unloved, I've been in good relationships in which I've been unhappy because I made my partner feel unloved. Maybe the universe just wants me to be alone for the rest of my life because I find relationships difficult. It's difficult because I've spent my whole life trying to find myself, overcome my crippling sadness, and the thought of having to do that whilst being responsible to provide someone a love I barely have in me is both hard and

35

overbearing. When I was alone it was okay because the only person, I could hurt was myself but being put in a position where I could hurt someone else is a heavy burden for a man that can barely stand up. A man that spends his life drowning in endless, meaningless pussy and never-ending pain with a huge dose of self-loathing. What a miserable life. But then again what is life? Sometimes I think that life is a sea of interchangeable waves, with days where the waves are easy to ride on and the sea is in tune with every little movement you make, and then you have days where the waves revolt and you fall overboard. But what do I know? I've never been on a surfboard in my life. Only thing I know in life is writing and fucking. I would say loving and women but that would require me to know what love is and how women work, in which I must admit my mind has failed me. It's the same vicious cycle. Whenever I lost one, I attracted another. Less love, more women. Why always more women? What was I trying to achieve? What was I running from? New women brought excitement into my pitiful life. The calls, the texts, the butterflies, first meetings, first kiss, first fuck. The sexual tension excited me, wondering how they looked naked, how they moaned, what turned them both on and off. Then later, slowly but surely, all their flaws would come to light and my mind would taint my love for them. I would still care for them, but my mind wouldn't allow my heart to love them. I would become more and more to them, and they would mean less and less to me.

I was once asked what love means and thinking about that question now, I think it means *pain*. With that being said I don't mean that the women in my life have caused me pain, but rather that pain is the only thing I've come to know in this life. Pain defined my childhood, described my adolescence, and explains my hatred for adulthood. But then again if love and pain are intertwined, and love as an action is needed in order to produce life, one could say pain has a beauty to it that doesn't make it tragic. There are days where I wish for love and days where I appreciate my solitude. I don't know, I've always been like that in a sense; love being alone but hate feeling lonely. It never felt right being alone. Most times it felt good, but *never* right. This is why I often question whether love was meant for me or if I've just been unlucky in my encounters with the opposite sex. I have a heart that's a hopeless romantic being controlled by a mind that's unloving. If I could provide you with any further explanation as to what that entails, I would, but that's just the problem I can't. Being unable to understand my mind made me afraid of it and being afraid of it made me incapable of embracing it. Maybe that's why I get infatuated and fall in love quicker than others, not necessarily because the love I'm seeking is genuine, but rather that love is a way of escape from the dreadful thought of being left alone with my mind. When you're with a woman they tend to do the thinking for you. What to eat. What to buy. What to do. I like that. Life is easy that way. It's hard to destroy your life when you have someone else thinking for you. In some way's women are my minds kryptonite, which is why I don't' think my mind likes it when I fall in love. The more I fall in love, the less control it has, and the less control it has the happier I am. I hate my *mind*.

3

I'm not sure when I first saw Célia DuPont. I think it was eleven years ago and I had just started studying law at Sorbonne Law School in Paris, trying to be an ordinary man in an *ordinary* world. An eighteen-year-old self-proclaimed anarchist that hated the legal system and what it represented was now studying to become a lawyer and carry on the proud values and principles of the French legal system. Some would laugh at the irony; others would pity my self-inflicted misery. Either way they were both right. I don't know why I chose law. I think it's because I was never good at math's and science, and I didn't care enough about money to study business. In the end law seemed attractive; imagine getting paid to talk shit and lie whiles people are forced to listen to you. In that sense there's a lot of similar traits between lawyers, poets and writers. I looked out of place walking in the hallway with my skateboard in my hand dressed in raggedy light blue bootcut jeans, black converses with a white star on them, a white graphic tee and a light blue denim jacket with a red white and black Chicago Bulls trucker cap trying to cover up my mid-length dreads. I checked my phone and saw that I had ten more minutes until my corporate law lecture started, said fuck it and jumped on my board. Cruising through the half empty hallways tic tacking and doing ollies, it wasn't until I noticed that everybody had stopped whatever they were doing and now had their eyes fixated on me before I realized that something was wrong. I got off my board turned around and saw that two campus security officers had been running after me this whole time.

'You can't skate on campus.'

He sounded like he was worn out from all that running, with sweat slightly dripping from his bald head, and his uniform barely fitting his 5'9 stocky frame.

'Says who?'

'University guidelines. It clearly states that scooters are not allowed.'

'Wait what? But a skateboard is not a scooter though?!'

'Look, there's no point in arguing. Don't let us catch you on that board next time.'

I didn't even get to respond before they turned their backs on me and started walking. I threw both of my middle fingers up and aimed it at their backs.

'Hugo can be such a buzzkill sometimes.'

Without me noticing she had managed to snuck up beside me. I turned towards her and said, 'who the fuck is Hugo?'.

'The man with the bald head.'

'How do you guys know each other?'

'He is always kind to me; I don't know what you must've done to piss him off.'

'Hmm maybe if I had a good pair of breasts, pussy and a charming smile.'

'Do you always curse?'

'No. Sometimes I lie, but most times I don't talk. Anyways, I have to go. I got class.'

'I know. 11am corporate law, we're in the same class. My name is Célia by the way…'

'Cool…My name is Charles, but my friends call me Chuck.'

'Nice to meet you Chuck.'

As we were walking towards the main auditorium, I kept wondering what made her take interest in me. I didn't believe in anything, and I hated *everything*. I didn't have a way of life or a God, but I would be lying if I said I never tried to pray to the man upstairs. Sitting in the interrogation room at the police station charged with breaking and entering, for a brief second, I became the most religious man on earth. Not even the pope could challenge my faith. I got the charges dropped and forgot God until I needed him again. Sometimes I feel bad for God because if I was him, I would hate love too. He has the most one-sided love to ever exist. Religion has a funny way of being a necessity in times of need, but an alternative in times of prosperity. And yet here she was, taking interest in an *uninteresting* man. What do you want from me, Célia...?

After our lecture we went to the library and found a quiet spot in the back. Sitting across from me, she was of petite height with golden brown skin, and her frizzy afro hair was tied in a messy bun with strands of hair curling by her ears and neck, outlining a face that was imperfectly *perfect*. She had a petite shape with black high waisted denim jeans that revealed her curves, a white top, and an outworn black letter jacket topped off with a pair of work boots that gave her whole appearance a gritty and yet attractive look. Célia DuPont; a rockstar's muse. Being in her presence turned me on to the point where I struggled to concentrate on my work.

'Fuck this, I can't do this. Let's do something else.'

'Like what?'

'I don't know. We can climb up to the roof.'

'But that's not allowed.'

'If Adam and Eve can go against God, I think we can afford to break Hugo's fragile heart and tedious rules.'

'Okay fine, just let me finish reading this chapter.'

Célia studied business with law, which meant that we had one class together each week. I liked that. That meant I now had something to look forward to.

She finished reading her chapter closed her book and we packed our stuff. We took the elevator up to the seventh floor, went through the door that had a no entrance sign on it and pushed open the fire exit door. We climbed up the ladder and got up to the roof. I always liked rooftops; it was a form of escape from this world, a world I could never seem to fit in. We live in a *paper town* society where we spend our days talking about our dreams, hopes and goals without even knowing who we are. A society where we've lost the innocence of being a child but have yet to gain the knowledge of being an adult, and it seems like we're stuck in an awkward place where our future seems so far away and yet our life is moving so fast. A society where we showcase our happiness on social media but reveal our misery in front of the mirror. A society in which I always felt like an outsider. A rebel without a *cause*.

We walked around admiring the view until she turned towards me and stared at me.

'I've noticed you smile whenever you talk, but your eyes…They always seem so sad. Is it because of love?'

'More so the lack of. Love never seems to find me. What about you?'

'Once. A couple of years ago.'

'What happened?'

'He fell out of love, I guess. Either love was too much for him or I was. I don't know. Something was too much for him.'

'Do you think about him?'

'Sometimes.'

'Does it hurt?'

'Yes. But that's the thing about love; everybody tells you how great it is, but they forget to mention how much it *hurts*.'

'I like you, Célia.'

'I like you too, Chuck.'

I had kissed women before, but this was different. Standing in the middle of the rooftop with our arms around each other and our lips locked, it felt like we had known each other our whole lives. The touch from her lips made me feel like she knew every dark secret I had kept hidden from the world, and what my insecurities were. I felt naked, vulnerable, and yet I also felt *safe*. This was a sense of happiness I wasn't accustomed to. The happiness from being loved.

4

The more time I spent with her, the more love poems I wrote. She always had that effect on me. Being in her presence would numb my pain and breathe life into an otherwise dead soul. Her love felt like *Novocain*. And yet we couldn't be more different. Célia loved God, her family, parties, people and life. I was the total opposite. But for her I was willing to change. I was willing to do *anything*. Some days I would ask myself if that's what love is, losing yourself in order to be with someone else. As time went on, I saw a different side of her. A side I *hated*. Our dissimilar views on everything led to heated arguments and days filled with silence treatment. The arguments would end with me apologizing, not because I was genuinely sorry but rather due to the fact that I couldn't stand it. I couldn't stand her shouting or being silent. See what Célia had in common with most women in our generation, was that she didn't know how to apologize or take accountability for her actions. Her anger replaced her beauty with ugliness and made me hate her presence. It was around 11am, I was halfway asleep, and my body was going through the initial stages of a hangover where it felt like someone was drilling a hole through my head. For a nineteen-year-old I drank as life had already worn me out.

'Chuck, wake up. Chuck.'

I loosely opened up my eyelids to see her standing over me with my phone in her hand. 'Huh, what is it?'

'Who is Sade, and why is she texting you saying that it was nice to meet you and that she would love to continue the conversation in person?'

'Why do you have my phone?'

'Because I was going to look at some of the pictures you took the other day. Anyways, answer my question.'

'I met her at the poetry reading I had at the student café last night.'

'Oh, so you're just giving your number out to random bitches now?'

She never cursed when she was happy but had the dirtiest vocabulary when she was angry. I never understood it. Some days it felt like I never understood *her*.

'She just wanted tips on her writing, that's all.'

'You know what, fuck you. You lying piece of shit! You're just like Matisse. No matter who you end up with, all men will do you wrong.'

She threw my phone on the bed, stormed out the bedroom and slammed the door behind her. During every argument she would compare me to her ex and mention how she blames herself for having the worst choice in men. I had never met the guy, but I hated him with passion. Fucking Matisse. I got up walked into the kitchen where I found her standing over the stove making pancakes and hugged her from behind.

'Look, I'm sorry if what I did hurt you. I'm never going to give out my number to other women again.'

She turned her body towards me to the point where our eyes met, 'Good, if you do it again, I'll kill you.'

I kissed her viciously before lifting her by her thighs and moving her over to the kitchen table. With her feet dangling off the table and my body in-between her legs, we continued kissing as I pulled down my boxers and slipped open her robe revealing her naked body and a floral red lace thong. I slid her panties to the side and put my cock in. With my arms supporting her back I started fucking her like a caveman that has never seen a woman before. Whenever I looked down after each stroke, I could see her cream all over my cock. I was determined to fuck Matisse out of her.

'Ahhh Chuck THAT FEELS SO FUCKING GOOD...let me take my panties off.'

'No. Leave them on.'

I turned her around as her robe fell to the ground, slid her panties to the side again and started ramming her from the back. She grabbed the end of the table to stabilize herself, as I was pulling her hair back. I gave her ten more strokes before I finally came. I went back into the bedroom to lay down and she went to the bathroom to clean herself up. She came back into the bedroom with a plate stacked with pancakes and a glass of orange juice. No matter how angry she was, she always made sure that I was fed. I hope Matisse never got this treatment.

'Chuck, me and the girls are going out tonight. Come out with us.'

'No, thanks. I'm good.'

'Please, come on. What are you even going to do today? Because I know you're not going to study.'

'I don't know. Skate, drink, write, I guess.'

'But that's what you always do.'

'That's what I want to do.'

'Oh pleaseee, I'm begging you. Do it for me.'

'Fine. But if I don't like it, I'm going back to my apartment.'

'Okay. Love you.'

Aside from sex, love never does us men any justice, having to cater to our girlfriends and do stuff we don't want to in order to avoid them ruining our lives.

Whoever created the rules to how love works must've been a woman that was *tired* of men.

I went to the store bought a six-pack of beer and went back to Célia's apartment. When I came back, Perin, Tanya and Lorraine were already in her living room drinking and talking. Perin and Lorraine were okay, but I disliked Tanya. She was one of those people that could never get their own relationship to work, so instead she spent time ruining other's. Whenever Célia and I would argue, Tanya would give her the worst advice which made me sometimes think if she hated me or didn't like seeing her friend happy. In the end I concluded that she just didn't like me. Which is fine because I didn't like her either. See Tanya was in a dysfunctional and toxic relationship with her on and off boyfriend Yousef. To the world they seemed like a young couple in love, but beneath the surface everything was wrong. Two fiery personalities that when caught at the wrong moment could put everyone around them in danger. They tried to mask their toxic love by posing as a couple that enjoyed lavish vacations, materialistic items and everything good life had to offer. But after being in their presence a couple of times, it wasn't hard to discover that they were just two lost souls desperately holding on to a fading love and using old memories to keep ablaze a dying flame. I cracked open a can of beer and sat on the couch next to Célia. I sat on my phone whiles they continued talking. They touched on the topic of sex and men.

'I'm about to text Olivier and ask if he wants to have sex later on tonight.'

They all started laughing except Lorraine who shook her head and sighed, 'Perin, you're actually crazy. How can you just approach someone like that? Doesn't sex mean anything to you?'. Perin had now turned her attention towards Lorraine and they engaged in a *mildly* interesting conversation.

'Why? Why do we always have to make sex out to be something it's not. Sex is not special. Sex is just sex. If we both know we want to fuck each other, what's the point of doing unnecessary small talk and going on dates when we're just going to end up sleeping with each other and never speak again.'

'Because sex is the most intimate act you can do with someone, so why not do it with someone you love? At least then it'll be special and romantic. If I know I don't love a man, I wouldn't feel comfortable with him seeing me naked.'

'No Lorraine, you're wrong. You don't need love in order to fuck. Sex is an act; love is a *choice*. Throughout history society has viewed sex as a rebellious act and yet we proceed to give it rules, instructions and labels. It's ridiculous.'

'I don't know Perin. I just feel like our generation has taken the meaning out of everything nowadays. Marriage, sex, love. It doesn't feel the same anymore. We no longer seek happiness or peace, and we don't work for love anymore. Instead, we use sex as an escape from our problems. We struggle for years to find someone to be in a relationship with, but we can *easily* find someone to fuck any day of the week. It just doesn't make sense.'

I sat there admiring Perin's directness and bravery. Shaming a woman for being vocal about her sexual desires or showing an intent to pursue a man is one of societies greatest sins, with another sin being that men should do the chasing and a woman is just left waiting until the man is ready. Either we overestimate a man's courage, or we degrade a woman's right to sexual freedom, no matter how we look at it, it's still wrong. Passion is a beast you can't control, and sex is a dance between passionate souls. Perin was a fiery redheaded nympho who loved fucking more than love. She caught my attention and her choice of clothing turned me on. She looked titillating sitting there in her black boots, fishnet stockings, red leather skirt topped off with a white top and matte lipstick. A part of me thought about what a great fuck she would be in bed. She seemed like the type that would let you do anything, and yet she had the appeal of a woman that had already done *everything*. Whiles Lorraine was a religious brunette that was saving herself for marriage. There was nothing *special* about her.

Célia and Tanya were talking about school related work, when Célia's phone rang. From the corner of my eye, I could see the phone screen. It was an incoming call from Matisse. I waited to see if she was going to answer it before I said anything. Oddly enough to my dismay she let the call go to voicemail. It was a test of our love and she *failed*. If she didn't have anything to hide why didn't she pick up the call. I sat upright from my slouched position and turned my body towards her.

'Why didn't you pick up, and why is he calling you at this time. Matter of fact why is he even calling you?'.

She had an uncomfortable look on her face, as the room went silent with a sense of awkwardness lingering in the air.

'Chuck not now. We can talk about it later.'

'No. I want to talk about it now.'

Tanya decided to join our conversation with a passive aggressive tone in her voice. 'Look Chuck, if she doesn't want to talk about it then leave her alone. You're not her dad.'

'Tanya how about you mind your own business, I was talking to Célia, not you. And Célia why does she always have to defend you; can you not speak for yourself?'.

Célia went silent as Tanya continued speaking on her behalf.

'Listen here you dickhead I'm her best friend, I was here before you and I'll be here *after* you. I can defend her and speak on her behalf however much I want!'

She was starting to piss me off. 'Tanya the only thing faker than your personality is your relationship, and the only thing faker than that is your awful nose job. How about you clean up your own shit, before you come crap in my backyard.'

Everybody could see her pale face redden, as she was switching between staring at me and Célia. 'WHAT THE FUCK CÉLIA, why did you tell him about my nose job. That was something private I told you! AND FUCK YOU CHUCK!! Say one more word and I'll smash this fucking bottle on your head right now!'

Lorraine and Perin were now talking to a crying Tanya as they tried to calm her down, whiles Célia was facing the dilemma of having to choose between her best friend or her boyfriend.

'I'm so sorry Tanya, I really am. It was just something that slipped out of me one day. And Chuck, come with me right now!'. We walked into the bedroom and locked the door. I sat on the edge of the bed with her standing a couple feet away from me.

'What the fuck is wrong with you, Chuck. You did not have to speak to her like that.'

'She started it. I've never liked her, and I never will. You're my girlfriend, not her. And yet every time something happens between us, she feels like she can add her two cents.'

'She's my friend Chuck, that's what friends do.'

'Anyways, why was Matisse calling you, and how long has this been going on?'

'We have been texting and calling for a couple of weeks. He is depressed and I'm just helping him get through it.'

'Oh ok. So, if I was to text and call other girls, I've been with in the past without you knowing, would that be okay with you?'

'Chuck you can't compare those two, and what do you mean? You have random girls texting you all the time. And I've been to your poetry readings, I know how you act around your little groupies, so don't even give me that bullshit!'

'But those are not girls I've fucked or loved.'

Tears started streaming down from her eyes and her voice became fragile and filled with *sadness*. Usually whenever I saw her cry, I would feel bad but tonight I didn't care.

'You know what Chuck, I'm tired...'

'Tired of what?'

'All *this*. Everyday there's a new issue, and every week is filled with arguments. I'm tired Chuck, I don't know if I can do this anymore...'

'So, what do you want to do...?'

She was busy wiping away tears with her hands, ruining her mascara. 'I don't know. I don't know what I want...I don't know if I need a break...space...I don't know. But I need something, because this is honestly too much.'

'I'm just going to leave'.

'Wow, so you don't want to talk about this?'

'There's nothing to talk about. You don't need to say much in order for something to be understood.'

'Okay Chuck, as always you do whatever you want...'

She sat on the bed as she continued crying with both of her palms covering her face. I stood up walked out the bedroom, put the remaining three cans of beer in a plastic bag, picked up my skateboard and headed out without speaking to anyone. I checked my phone. It was 10.30pm. I jumped on my board, skated down to the nearest corner shop and bought a bottle of Yellow Tail white chardonnay. Came out of the shop, checked my phone again. It was 10.50pm. I went through my contacts until I found Sade's number.
Ring...ring...ring...ring...She answered.

'Hello?'

'Hey, it's Charles from the poetry reading the other night.'

'Hey Charles, I remember your voice. How are you?'

'I'm okay. Could be better, could be worse.'

'You had a rough evening or something?'

'No. Well yes kind of. The usual evening, I guess. I just felt it more this time. What about you, what are you up to tonight?'

'Oh okay. Not much, was just going to do some writing I think.'

'Well, I got a bottle of wine I don't want to drink alone, and a *mild* sadness I want to forget. Mind keeping me company?'

'Okay, if you promise to help me with my writing.'

'Your wish is my command, Sade.'

'Cool. Do you smoke weed?'

'Not usually, but tonight I will.'

'Ok cool, I'll bring a joint. Do you want me to come to yours?'

'Yes. I'll text you the address.'

'Ok. See you soon.'

'Bye.'

I hung up texted her my address and skated back to my apartment. I hurriedly cleaned up my place. Threw away empty pizza boxes, washed the plates in my sink, put my dirty clothes in the laundry basket, folded the clean clothes on my couch and hoovered the place. Staring at my clean apartment, it seemed like your typical student studio. I didn't have much, but I had enough. I had a queen-sized bed, a bathroom, a grey couch, a grey carpet that covered the whole floor, a 30inch tv that was connected to my PlayStation, a midsized closet and a small kitchen. The walls were brown brick walls, which gave the whole studio a New

York esque look...well from what I had at least seen of New York in movies and tv-series. The rest of the apartment was decorated with two plants and my little bonsai tree, a poster of James Dean and 2Pac, my five half decent paintings that were placed in different parts of the apartment and a small bookshelf that was cut out in the wall and consisted of my minor collection of classical books.

It was 11.56pm I checked my phone and saw that I had received a text from Sade five minutes ago. Fuck. I need to stop putting my phone on do not disturb mode. I took the elevator down to the ground floor and opened up the door. It was autumn in Paris, and she was dressed accordingly. She had on a black denim jacket with graffiti sprayed on it, light blue denim jeans that covered parts of her white sneakers and were split half open by the knees, a red crop top, gold chain hanging around her neck and rings spread across her fingers. She was slim with a light skin complexion, with her beach curly hair swaying in the autumn breeze, her plump pinkish lips and her picturesquely shaped eyes highlighting a beautiful golden-brown color. I wish Célia could see her beauty.

'Hey sorry, I forgot to check my phone.'

'No problem, your door was keeping me entertained anyways.'

She had a sense of humor. I liked that. We got in the elevator I pressed number 4, and we stood there in silence. Me looking at myself in the mirror, and her being busy on her phone. Watching my reflection in the mirror, I had on my converses, khaki pants, a black Jimi Hendrix tee and a black beanie. I looked at my eyes, they seemed miserable. I felt miserable. And yet here I was standing in the elevator with a beautiful woman that wanted to spend time with me. I guess sadness must be a part of my *charm*. We got out the elevator walked down the hallway and entered my apartment. She took off her shoes and walked around the apartment, I went to the fridge took out a beer and sat on the couch facing the tv.

'I can see you read a lot of *Charles Bukowski*'. She was browsing through my books.

'He's my favorite author. I like to think that I was named after him.'

'What about him do you like?'

'His honesty, I think. And I like how everything he writes seems so unfiltered. Great writer indeed. You don't have a lot of them nowadays.' I took another sip of my beer as a toast to Bukowski. Your authenticity is truly missed in this fraudulent world.

'Who else do you like reading?'

'*Hank Moody*. I like his writing. The way it flows, he makes it seem so effortless. Almost like poetry. What about you?'

'He's not that known, but I really like *Lawrence Savage*. I love the way he incorporates his poetry into his writing, it's almost like art. And if you don't pay attention, you'll miss them, but when you find them it will give the chapter a whole new meaning.'

'Who is he?'

'An up-and-coming writer from England. He wrote a book called Love me, Justice. You should check him out. And check out some of his poetry books too, my favorite one of his is Heartbreak & Me'.

'What does he write about?'

'He writes about a lot of stuff but most of his writing is centered around love, heartbreak, pain and how he never seems to find a place for himself in this world.

I've read your poems on your online blog. Your work and your writing are quite similar to his.'

'Cool. I'll check him out. Do you want a glass of wine?'

'How about we smoke first?'

'That works too.'

I had a tall casement window by the right-hand side of my bed that looked down towards a park with a cathedral in the middle of it, and across from it you had a busy high street consisting of cheap hotels, clubs, chicken shops, corner shops and a decent amount of drug dealing at night. The area was okay, but the monthly rent on the apartment was too good to pass up. I preferred this side of Paris anyways. I felt comfortable here. Amongst the middle-class workers, the loners and the *outcast* of society. You can be whoever you want, dress however you want and do whatever you want. Rich areas and high-end restaurants made me uneasy. A community where those around you judge you, and the thickness of your wallet defines you. I pity the rich. Spending all that money to run away from us poor people, just to find themselves in a worse environment. An environment filled with their *kind*.

With the window wide open, we sat on the ledge looking out towards the street that was packed with people. It was a Saturday night and Parisians were wide awake drowning in a sea of alcohol and horniness as the sky was clouded with stars. She lit up the joint and we took turns smoking.

She blew out smoke from the side of her mouth, handed me the joint and looked at me. 'Your room. Its creative and yet empty. In a way it resembles you.' I held the joint in my hand, inhaled it and blew out. I stared back.

'I don't know if that's a compliment or an insult.'

'It's whatever you want it to be. There's a certain sadness in your eyes that makes you handsome. Poetic handsomeness, almost. If that's a word. I don't know. You just seem different from most guys.'

'I'm in pain, they're just content. It gives me an extra edge over those fools.'

She let out a smile that made her eyes squint and her cheekbones rise. A smile that told me that I was doing something *right*.

'Oh, look at that. Who knew the thought of my pain would be the key to your heart?'

'Well how many men do you know that use their sadness to seduce a woman?'

'Using misery to keep a woman in your life is one of man's greatest magic tricks. That's the secret to the art of flirting.'

'The other night you read a bunch of love poems. Were they all about the same girl?'

'Yes.'

'Who?'

'Célia.'

'Are you guys together?'

'Not really. Well, I don't know. I think I'll find out tomorrow. What about you, are you in love?'

'I write about it, but I don't practice it.'

'Why not?'

'I don't know. Never found it, I guess. I've had good men, but none of them were right.'

'Well, who knows. You might find it tonight.'

'With a man that still writes love poems about a girl that he doesn't know whether to call ex or girlfriend? I don't think so.'

'I have a big heart, Sade. There's more than enough room for you in it.'

'I don't know. We'll see.'

We finished the joint and she went and sat on the couch. I put on music, went to the kitchen counter opened up the bottle of chardonnay picked up two wineglasses and walked back to the couch. I sat down next to her. She handed me her phone to show me her poetry. Her poems were about how men take advantage of her love, being the black sheep in her family, how much she hates this generation, her experiences with depression, and her losing her friend to suicide a couple of years ago. She had been through a lot for a twenty-year-old woman. In terms of her writing, the potential was there, she just needed to work more on her craft.

'Your poetry is good. I liked the one you titled Unfinished. It was a beautiful way to describe a girl that found it difficult to fit into society, into her family and her struggle to believe in love again after her first heart break. The writing is good, but it's missing something.'

'Like what? What is it missing?'

'I don't know. A certain rawness, I guess. Don't be afraid to be vulnerable when you're writing. Let the reader feel your pain, sadness, tears, anger. Let them feel everything. Poetry isn't about how you write, it's about what you can make others *feel*.'

'You really know what you're talking about huh. Do you have plans on publishing anything?'

'I have a collection of poems I'm trying to put together, and I'm currently working on my first novel.'

'Ouuu that's exciting. What is the novel called?'

'I don't know yet. You'll be the first one to find out when I have the name ready.'

'Okay. Don't forget me when you're famous, Charles.'

I put my arm around her as I stared into her eyes. 'I'll bring you with me. And call me Chuck.'

I don't know if it was the weed, the alcohol or a combination of both but kissing her felt more intense than usual. She sat on top of me as we continued kissing and undressing each other. She took off her denim jacket. I reached down and took off her socks. She took off my tee. I took off her crop top. She wasn't wearing a bra underneath. I started sucking on her nipples, constantly switching from one boob to another. Her pair of swooping breasts fit perfectly into my mouth. She stood up and took off her jeans to reveal a white lace thong underneath, went on her knees and started unbuckling my belt. I gave her a hand and took off my khaki pants and boxers and kicked them to the side. She went on her knees again put both hands around my cock and started sucking. I grabbed her hair as I watched her head in a constant motion going up and down. Up. Down. Up. Down. She gathered up enough saliva, spat it back on my cock and continued the motion. Up. Down. Up. Down. One hand. Two hand. It felt great. I wanted to explode in her mouth, but I had to restrain myself.

'Ahhhh Ahhh FUCKK ME...come sit on it.'

'Okay. Let me take my panties off.'

'No. Leave them on.'

She sat on my cock and resumed the motion with her body. Up. Down. Up. Down. With one hand on her ass and the other on her back, I pushed her towards me as I started thrusting. I could feel her breasts pressing up on my face. I fucked her like I've never had sex before. Slow strokes. Fast strokes. All kinds of strokes. At one point I didn't know if I was fucking her or trying to fuck out the anger in me. The anger caused by Célia. Either way I couldn't complain. We moved over to the bed. I laid behind her as I lifted her leg up and slid my cock in. I started thrusting again. Slow strokes. Fast strokes. Her leg came down, and I took the arm that was free and was switching between choking her and turning her face around to kiss me.

'AHHH YOU LIKE THAT?'

'YES, BABY DON'T STOP...It feels so fucking good...'

I didn't last for long before I could feel my cock wanting to explode.

'AHHH...I'M CUMMING I'M CUMMING'.

'COME FOR ME BABY...Ahhhh there you go...ahhh.'

She stood up from the bed. With sweat dripping from my forehead, I laid there admiring her naked body.

'Did you cum?'

'No. But I was close.'

She put on my Jimi Hendrix tee and walked towards the bathroom. Well at least one of us got *off*. I opened my pack of cigarettes and went to the ledge. The air was cool, and the otherwise busy street was now starting to fall asleep. I finished and went back to bed. She came back from the bathroom and laid down close to me. We kissed for a bit before she turned away with my one arm over her head and the other wrapped around her body fondling her breasts. First, she slept. Then I slept. With the music still playing in the background. The morning after I woke up *alone* with the sun piercing my eyes. I turned away from the sun and checked my phone. It was 12.15pm. I had five missed calls. They were all from Célia. Half-awake I called her back.

'Hello.' She was angry.

'Hey, it's Chuck.'

'What have you been up to, I've tried calling you like fifteen times or so. I was worried after you left yesterday.'

'I'm okay.'

'How are you?'

'I'm okay. What about you?'

'I don't know, Chuck. I've done some thinking. And I think we need to talk.'

'Talk about what?'

'Us, Chuck. Us.'

'Okay. That's fine.'

'Where did you go last night?'

'Back to my apartment.'

'Were you alone?'

'Now I am. But not yesterday.'

'Who were you with?'

'A friend.'

'What friend? You don't have any here in Paris.'

'Now I do.'

'Okay. What's their name?'

'Sade.'

'FUCK YOU CHUCK!! YOU FUCKING ASSHOLE!!!
YOU CHEATING PIECE OF SHIT!! I'm done with you!
And I'm going to go fuck Matisse! I hope you have a
miserable life.'

'I love you too, Célia. And give Matisse my regards.'

She hung up. I guess she was angry. Matisse could have her for all I care. At least now I had Sade. A *friend* and a fuck, without any labels or annoying friends that didn't like me. The best combination possible. I put on a pair of boxers walked to the fridge, cracked open a beer, took out my laptop and sat on the couch. I wrote ten poems about heartbreak and the women that left me at some point in my life. My grandmother. My mother. Célia.

5

It had been around a year since I last spoke to Célia, and during that time a lot had changed. I dropped out of law school and decided to spend my time trying to become a writer. I guess there was no point in pursuing a law degree if you had no love for people, money, long office hours and suits. I hated suits. Every time I had to wear one it felt as if my soul was ripped away and I was stripped of my values and integrity. I wasn't necessarily a man of many principles, but I did have a *few*.

1. Be kind to those that provide a service to you. They are being paid to do their job, not endure your entitled bullshit.
2. Never look down on someone. No matter how important you think you are, most of us don't care.
3. Don't take life too seriously. The best memories are usually the most unplanned.
4. Be yourself. This world has enough people that die trying to be someone else.

5. Be grateful for those that love you. Because no one on this earth owes you anything.

I was now living in a three-bedroom apartment that I shared with two other people in Saint-Ouen-sur-Seine on the northside of Paris. The area was culturally vibrant and lively, with a mixture of different ethnicities and nationalities gelling together to create a diverse community. The apartment was right next to a Turkish restaurant called Cappadocia that served fast food, Mediterranean, European, Turkish and Middle Eastern cuisines. On the days where I couldn't gather enough energy and strength to cook dinner, you could always find me there. Usually switching between ordering a mix grill or a döner kebab, with mix grill being my favorite. Mix grill was a selection of lamb cutlet, diced chicken, diced lamb, lamb döner and lamb kofte skewered with onion, peppers and tomatoes, served with green leaves, red onion and bulgur. I soon became a regular and formed a relationship with the owners and a couple of the employees. The business had been in the same family since they migrated from Turkey to France during the Dersim rebellion, which was an uprising against the Turkish government in the Dersim region of eastern Turkey. The oldest child Aydin Dogan was running the restaurant and had been in charge ever since his father passed it down to him nine years ago. I liked Aydin. He was a forty-three-year-old man with a loving wife named Fatma and their three kids; Serhan their oldest was eighteen and just a couple of years younger than me. Diren was fifteen and Emira was nine. Aydin had a passion for literature and love, and he took great interest in my poetry, mainly those about love. You could tell by his relationship with Fatma that the *Gods* of love had been good to him. Even though they spent countless hours every day, evening and sometimes nights making food for others, they never got tired of being around each other. Sitting there watching them behind the counter, Aydin in the backroom cooking and Fatma sitting by the cash register I could just *imagine* what their love must feel like. A love that never gets old because it rejuvenates every morning when you wake up next to that person. A love where your soul feels complete in their presence. Would I ever find a love like *that*?

Serhan was walking towards the counter with empty plates in his hand, 'Yuck, can you guys stop. There are people here you know.'

Aydin slightly loosened his grip around Fatma's waist removed his lips away from hers and turned towards Serhan.

'I don't care. My restaurant my rules. They can love my food and I can love my woman. You young people don't appreciate love anymore, or am I wrong Chuck?'

With my mouth half full of food, I turned my face around, 'You're totally right Aydin. I appreciate this mix grill much more.'

Aydin laughed. I laughed. We all laughed.

I liked Serhan too. After finishing high school, he decided to stay and help his parents run the business instead of attending university. He dreamt of one day having his own chain of restaurants spread across the world and would always tell me about his future plans for their family restaurant. Serhan was hardworking, caring and had a kind heart. We didn't have much in common, but I appreciated his *genuineness*. I was attempting to teach him how to skateboard, and he was trying to make me like football. His favorite team was Liverpool, and his favorite player was Cristiano Ronaldo. It wasn't easy at all. He was struggling to balance on a board, and I was having difficulties grasping the concept and importance of football. As time went on, he ended up buying his own skateboard, and I must say I did become slightly interested in the sport. We even watched a couple of games together on one of the tv's they had in the restaurant.

Alcohol isn't cheap and neither is living, which meant that I had to get a job in order to afford my rent and my fondness for drinking. I was no longer receiving student finance and at that time I was reading poems for free. My roommate Adrìan Mendez helped me secure a job as a library assistant at Paris Descartes University, where he studied psychology. I met Adrìan at a party a mutual friend of ours hosted.

I stepped outside on the porch for a smoke. Busy struggling to find my lighter and oblivious to the fact that I was no longer alone, Adrían took out his and handed it to me. We got to smoking and talking and found out we had a *lot* in common. Adrìan was a man with no family, few friends and filled with hate. We maintained contact and called each other three to four times a week. I soon developed a soft spot for Adrian, and he would often seek my advice regarding his relationship and my company whenever he was angry or sad. In some ways I understood *him* better than I understood myself. When I told him about my plan to drop out of university, he was quick in asking me to come live with him and his girlfriend. The job at the university was alright. I worked twelve-hour shifts starting 8pm and finishing 8am four days a week every Monday, Wednesday, Friday and Sunday. Aside from sitting at the helpdesk and helping students with their enquiries I was free to do whatever I wanted. I spent most of my time working on my novel and reading.

It was Tuesday evening, and I was making my up to the apartment with a takeaway box from Cappadocia in my left hand and my skateboard in the other. It had been a *good* day spent at the park. Skating, drinking and falling. My legs were sore, and my body felt heavy as I struggled to climb the stairs up to the third floor. The thought of having an elevator made me miss my old apartment. I guess being a student had its perks. I made my way into the apartment put the takeaway box on the kitchen table, walked into my room leaned my skateboard up against the wall near the door and threw myself on the bed. I hadn't been on my phone the whole day. I took it up from my right front pocket looked at the time it was 7.45pm. Saw that I had seven missed calls from my grandmother, five from my mother and three from Célia. I called back Célia. The phone rang for a while before she finally picked up.

'Chuck! Are you okay?'

'I'm good. What's wrong?'

'Your grandma has been trying to call you. You need to call her back now.'

'I know. I saw the missed calls. I will call her tomorrow or next week or so.'

'Chuck, stop! You need to call her now! It's important.'

'Why? What's happened?'

'It's about Henry.'

'What about Henry?'

'I think it's better if your grandma tells you. I'm so sorry Chuck...'

I hung up. My stomach felt tense. The same feeling, I had when I sat in the holding cell waiting to be interrogated. I took a couple of deep breaths before I dialed my grandmother's phone number.

'Charles! I've tried calling you.'

'I know. I saw the missed calls. What happened to Henry?'

'Charles, I don't know how to say this...'

'Say what?'

I could hear her cry. 'Henry's dead, Charles....He died around 2 o'clock.'

'How did he die?'

'Car accident. The car Henry was in got hit from the passenger side. Henry was in the passenger seat. He died on impact...'

'Okay.'

'Charles I'm so sorry, please come home baby. I love y-'

I hung up. Stood up from the bed and walked over to the bathroom. Sat down against the wall, held my knees close to my face with my arms and started crying. The faster I cried the more it felt as if someone was twisting the insides of my stomach with their bare hands. It was *painful*. Henry was the first person I befriended when we moved to France and the person, I had the most love for in this world. Growing up in a neighborhood where we didn't have much, we always had each other, and experienced everything *together*.

Adrían heard me crying and rushed into the bathroom.

'Chuck! You okay?? What's wrong?'

With tears flooding down from my eyes I was too embarrassed and ashamed to look at him. The result of being raised by a grandmother who would often remind me that crying is a sign of *weakness*. With my head down I struggled to put together words in an attempt to reply back.

'It's...Henry...He's dead.... HE FUCKING DIED...'

He sat down next to me and put his arm around my shoulder. I continued crying whiles he was silent. He didn't have to say much. Everybody that knew me on a *personal* level knew how much I loved Henry. For the remainder of that week, I didn't go to work, shower, write or skate. I didn't do anything aside from crying, *thinking* and drinking. Laying there on my bed surrounded by darkness as the memories I shared with Henry kept replaying in my head. I started thinking about the times we would steal from the local shop every morning just to have lunch at school. The times we almost got caught as we ran away with baguettes in our hands looking at each other smiling and laughing. When I got a Sunday job selling newspaper in the neighborhood and I would take the little money I earned and bought food for us the next day. When we were seven years old and the principle at our elementary school choked and slammed me up against the wall, and Henry filled with rage started attacking him. When we were fourteen years old running from the police after breaking into a home and Henry shouting at me to continue running as he stopped and got arrested. When I sat at the police station nervous and scared and he had his arm around my shoulder looked me in the eyes and told me that everything was going to be okay. When I showed him my poetry for the first time, and he told me that I would become a great writer and we would move out to Los Angeles together. Last time we spoke was one month after Célia and I broke up and I experienced suicidal thoughts. Henry stayed on the phone with me every night until I slept even though he had work in the morning, just to make sure that I didn't do anything. Nobody understood my pain and loved me the *way* he did. In a life filled with misery, Henry was my only *blessing*.

It was Friday around 3.15pm. I sat on my bed reading the messages between me and Henry when I got an incoming call. It was from Célia.

'Hello.'

'Hi Chuck...Are you okay?'

'I don't know...Don't think so'

'Have you been eating?'

'No. Not really.'

'What have you been doing?'

'Nothing really.'

'Aww Chuck please take care of yourself, and please try to eat...I know how much you loved Hen-'

'What do you want?'

'I spoke with your grandma earlier today. The funeral is on Monday. I can call in sick and drive you, if you want?'

'I don't think I'm going.'

'Chuck, I know this is hard for you, but please don't do this. Please go. I'll come pick you up on Monday, okay?'

'Okay.'

'Do you still live in the same apartment?'

'No.'

'Where do you live now?'

'Saint-Ouen.'

'Okay. Text me your address and I'll come get you in the morning on Monday.'

'Okay.'

'I love you, Chuck.'

'Okay.'

She hung up.

The night before the funeral I had difficulties sleeping.
There were empty beer cans laying around the floor in
the room. I checked my phone it was 3am. I had been
continuously drinking the whole day. I don't know how
much I had spent on beer that week. To be honest I
didn't care. I sat upright at the edge of my bed
stretched my arm out and took out another beer from
the pack, cracked it open and took a sip then cried. I
continued the process as I found myself recalling a
conversation between me and Henry the night before I
left Reims to move to Paris. We sat on the bench in the
middle of the playground in our neighborhood with our
bodies facing the moon. It was around 2.30am with the
cool summer air allowing us to be in light clothing.
Sitting there in a Nike tracksuit and running his hand

through his kinky and coily hair, he opened a pack of cigarettes and handed me one.

'Can't believe you're leaving man. Things won't be the same without you.'

'I don't know. I just feel like it's time for me to leave. You know sometimes in life comfort brings you peace but only the unknown will grant you *growth*.'

He looked at me started laughing and shook his head, 'You and your fucking philosophical words, now what's that supposed to mean?'

'I don't know man, like in order to grow as a person you need sometimes do what makes you uncomfortable or might seem scary.'

'So, what, you're afraid of Paris?'

'No afraid of the city, but more so what's going to happen. What about you, don't you want to leave Reims?'

'Look around Chuck. Croix Rogue is the only place I *know*, and I don't know about you, but I like being places where I'm comfortable. Plus, I got my court date coming up soon.'

'What is your lawyer saying?'

'Nothing much, he's saying I'll be okay. But then again, I'm just another case he's going to forget regardless of the outcome, so I don't know. They don't have much evidence on me anyways asides from a couple of grams and a stack of money. I just felt bad for my mom since she was there when the apartment got raided.'

'You'll be good man. Just keep your head up and let me know if you need anything. How's your mother doing?'

'Not good. She lost her job at the kindergarten, and Saïd just got diagnosed with ME.'

'What's that?'

'Chronic fatigue syndrome. We're looking at treatment plans, but they're all so fucking expensive. What world do we live in where you have to pay to treat an illness you didn't *choose* to have?'

'A *cruel* one.'

'Tell me about it, man. I'm even thinking about getting a job at Abdi's shop to help my mom with the bills.'

'Ohhh look at that. Henry Mohamud a workingman.'

'Charles Johnson a soon to be lawyer that hates police. Guess the world is filled with irony.'

We kept laughing as we stood up stomped our cigarettes and started walking back towards our apartment block. On the way back he paused as he turned his body towards me and pat me on my arm.

'By the way Chuck, Bayram told me Lisa is single again. I know how much you've been crushing on her ever since second grade. You should text her.'

'So that Habib can come fight me? Nahh man. You know how sensitive Habib is, imagine how emotional he would be about Lisa.'

'I know for a fact you can beat up Habib. But you're right, he can be a sensitive bitch sometimes. Remember when he ran after Tariq with a knife because Tariq said his head was shaped like an alien?'

We started laughing before he stopped and looked at me with a serious face. 'But honestly Chuck, I'm going to miss you. Shit won't be the same without my partner in crime.'

'I'm going to miss you too, Henry. Paris is just an hour or so away, just come whenever you feel like it.'

'I will. Call me when you arrive tomorrow and tell the girls in Paris that Henry is coming for them. Just promise me you'll never forget where you came from and don't lose yourself. Because Paris will do that to you.'

'Never man. How could I ever forget your ugly face and Croix Rogue?'

We laughed again gave each other a hug and started walking our separate ways before he turned around and shouted, 'I LOVE YOU MON FRÈRE...'

I shouted back. 'I LOVE YOU TOO BROTHER....' walked into apartment number *36* and shut the door behind me.

I was busy wiping away tears when my alarm went off. It was 6.30am and Célia would be here in an hour. I stood up walked into the bathroom. Took a crap, showered, brushed my teeth and walked back into the room. I was contemplating whether I should iron my white shirt or not until I picked up my phone to check the time. It was 7.20am. Fuck. I put on the rumpled suit and stood in front of the mirror as I struggled to fix my tie. Adrian came in and stood by the door entrance.

'Hey man. Do you need help with your tie?'

I nodded my head and handed it to him.

'How are you feeling Chuck? You okay?'

'I don't know. I don't think so.'

'You know Chuck sometimes death can be more *peaceful* than existing.'

'How so...?'

'This world we live in with its standards and requirements has made it impossible for us to obtain peace. From the time we are born, we are forced to mold ourselves into how society wants us to be. We are told what to do, how to act and how to live a normal life. But the truth is that this life is not normal. We spend countless years working to the point where we forget what living feels like. That's the beauty of *death*. Dying is us breaking free from the chains of society and the *bondage* this world has over us. Death has no rules, expectations, or requirements. Death is eternal peace, whiles living is a *hopeless* pursuit of that peace.'

I continued nodding my head in silence.

'You'll be okay, Chuck. It's okay to cry, to be sad...it's okay to *not* be okay. There, the tie should be good now. I have to go get ready for class but call me later and let me know how the funeral went. Remember you can talk to me about anything and I'm always here for you.'

He left the room, and I sat on the edge of the bed to put on my dress shoes. I started thinking about what Adrian said, and he was right. I had spent my whole life longing for a peace I was starting to question if I would ever find on this earth. These days life as an adult got me wishing for a rebirth, with thoughts about my future clouded with fear and my mind overwhelmed with responsibilities. Being alone with my mind would always bring forth my insecurities, which is why I kept myself busy trying to achieve things that never made me happy. Regrets about my past would turn to doubts about my future, the same way how laughter when I'm around company would turn to sorrow whenever I'm alone.

I heard a knock at the door, looked up and saw that it was Célia. She had on a knee length black dress with short sleeves that had a figure-hugging cut and was topped off with a pair of black heeled court shoes and a slim gold watch on her right wrist.

'Hey, you ready? Some girl let me in.'

'It's Esther, my roommate's girlfriend.'

'Ohh okay. How are you feeling?'

'I don't know. Honestly Célia I just want to die. I'm tired. Tired of feeling sad, in pain. I'm just tired of being *alive*.'

She walked over and sat close enough to put her arm around me. I don't know if it was her touch, being in her presence *again* or the grief I had been feeling, but a rush of sudden sadness overcame me, and I laid my head on her lap as I started crying. She kept stroking my arm as she whispered, 'It's okay, Chuck...everything will be okay...'

After a while I rose up and wiped away the tears, 'Let's go.'

'Are you sure, Chuck? Just take your time. We don't have to leave now.'

'I'm ready.'

'Okay. Let's go.'

Her car was parked on the street in front of my apartment building. She drove a red 3-door hatchback Peugeot 108. We got in the car and started the one hour and thirty minutes journey from Paris to Reims. She turned down the volume on the radio and was switching between staring at me and the road.

'Have you been drinking?'

'Yes.'

'I can tell. You need to stop drinking so much. Remember that you have a heart problem.'

'I know.'

'How did your last appointment go?'

'It went fine. They did an EKG test and the doctor told me that I would have to come in for yearly checkups since there are concerns that my heart might grow in the future.'

'I don't know how that's fine, but okay. Just make sure to listen to whatever they say and cut out all this smoking and drinking. Take care of yourself Chuck. Remember that your granddad died of heart atta-'

'I don't want to talk about him.'

'I wasn't going to talk about him. I'm just telling you to be careful. Your grandma called me yesterday, she said she can't come to the funeral.'

'She *never* liked Henry anyways. I wasn't expecting anything less from that woman.'

'Don't say that... She misses you and loves you though...your mom misses you too. You haven't even called her back...'

'If loving someone means hurting them, then yes, her and my mother must love me dearly.'

'Chuck, I know you're grieving but stop being childish. At some point you'll have to grow up and talk with them about these issues instead of *running* away from your problems.'

'We'll see. What about you, how you been?'

'I've been okay. Just been a stressful couple of months. Elizabeth is pregnant and I've been helping her plan out her wedding. Who knew being maid of honor would mean so much work?'

'Wow. Can't believe your sister is pregnant.'

'I know right. Crazy to believe that I'm going to be an aunt soon.'

'Makes me think about all the conversations we had about children.'

She started laughing, 'The fact that we even had a list of baby names. I still remember the time you got upset because I didn't like your suggestion. What was the name again?'

'I think it was Rakim.'

We continued laughing before she turned up the volume on the radio to cover up the uncomfortable silence that followed.

It wasn't until I felt the force of someone pushing me before I opened up my eyes.

'Chuck...Chuck...wake up...We're here.'

I rubbed my eyes looked outside the passenger window and saw that we were back in Paris. I must've passed out as soon as we got back in the car after the funeral. It felt strange going back home to the city where I was raised, thinking about all the people I've met, tears I cried and the laughs I had there. Watching Henry's coffin being lowered into the ground made me realize that loving someone else means accepting every aspect of them without no form for *judgement*. The good and the *bad*. Henry was there when I was innocent, cold hearted, and when I was trying to change. He gave me a chance at love and forgave all my wrongs. A chance I never gave to those around me.

'You're right.'

She had now turned off the car engine and was facing me.

'About what?'

'About my grandmother and my mother. I need to forgive them. I never opened up my heart to give them a chance to right their wrongs.'

'That's good, Chuck. I'm proud of you. What made you come to that conclusion?'

I took a hold of her hand that was free, 'Thinking about Henry...and you...'

'Me?'

'I'm sorry, Célia...For the wrongs I did, the hurt I caused you...for everything... I *need* you Célia...'

When she spoke, her clear tone was undercut with a choking heaviness that forced her to pause several times and every word she uttered was full of sadness.

'That's the first time an apology from you ever felt *real*...and I'm sorry too. I wasn't always the girlfriend you needed me to be...I never tried to understand your pain...which meant that in a way I could never understand you...I learned that sadness is not an emotion for you Chuck. It's a constant *state* of mind you live in. That was my mistake. Thinking that I could love your depression *away*...'

She was right. A misconception that is often made by those that get into a relationship with someone that suffers from depression is that they think their love can *cure* their partner's mental illness. You can't love someone's mental illness away. But you can love them through it, with it and you can love them on bad days, good days, *nothing* days and everything days. That's the only type of love they want from you. Love of *acceptance*.

We stared at each other in silence. Looking into her teary eyes and my hand holding hers it dawned on me how much I loved this woman. How the thought of her would cause an inferno in my heart, and her presence being a *safe haven* from all my storms. How she was not only the guardian of my peace but also the gatekeeper to my happiness. I put my hand on her face and drew her close to me. We kissed and yet it felt as if there was an emotional wall that created distance between us. It felt as if I was kissing someone or *something* that had died. She pushed herself back and removed her hands from mine.

'I can't do this Chuck...I can't go back.'

'I miss you Célia...I can't do this without you. I need you.'

'I miss you too...but we're not good for each other Chuck. And it would be unfair.'

'What would be unfair?'

'This. To go back to this. You can't expect me to allow you back into my life just because you *apologized*...'

'You're right. I understand.'

'I don't want to look dumb Chuck...in front of my family...my friends...for Christ sakes you cheated on me!'

She turned her face away and was looking out the window whiles I stared at the floor trying to accept the painful truth; that she was *gone* for good.

'I love you Chuck, and I will always do. But I can't go back to you...you have to find that *completeness* in yourself instead of seeking it in other women. You can't always fuck your mommy issues away Chuck. You always tell me that you're not scared of anything...and yet you've spent your whole life running away from *yourself*.'

For the first time ever since we met, I felt like a *stranger* in her presence. A stranger that had overstayed his welcome. 'You're right, Célia. I understand...' I opened up the passenger door making my way out as she kept shouting after me 'CHUCK...Chuck!! Come back!' I closed the door and walked away.

Walking out of the car I felt empty. I didn't know where to go or what to do. In the end I walked into Cappadocia. It was around 3.30pm and with most people still at work or school the restaurant was empty except for a couple of elderly customers and delinquent teenagers. I walked in and sat at the table close to the window that looked out towards the street and the hotel that was across the restaurant. Aydin came out from the kitchen and saw me, 'Chuck my man, look at you in a suit. Where did you come from?'

I replied back, 'A funeral...'

He came over and sat on the chair across from me.

'You okay, son?'

'I don't think so Aydin. I just buried my best friend and the girl I love doesn't love me *back*...'

'Which one hurts *more*?'

'The one about love.'

'Why?'

'Because I don't know if I will ever love someone that way again.'

'Do you want to hear a story?'

'Okay…'

'When I was around your age, I was with a woman named Selma. I was madly in love and was sure this was the woman I was going to marry and start a family with. But I found out later on that she didn't have the same undying love for me like I had for her. Which is why my heart was shattered when Selma told me she was moving to Germany to go study and didn't want any relationships holding her back in France. Basically, telling me that she wanted to go explore and live her life.'

'How did that make you feel?'

'I felt the same way how you're feeling now. Like shit man, pure shit. When my parents a couple of years later told me that they had chosen who I was going to marry I got angry. I was pissed that it wasn't Selma.

She was the only woman I *wanted* but I couldn't have. Now look twenty years later I'm still together with the woman I was arranged to marry, and I love her more than life itself. Who knows, maybe I still do love Selma, but I can guarantee you I found *better* love in Fatma. Did you know what that taught me?'

'No.'

'That when you refer to someone as your soulmate, you're insulting the magic of love. Love is a feeling, sensation and bond you can build with anyone as long as the *chemistry* is there. That's what makes it so special. How could you restrict your love to only one person when it can be extended to the whole world? Calling someone your soulmate is a slap in the face to love as an artform. Take me and Fatma for example. When we met each other on our wedding day we didn't know each other at all. But through time we ended up building an eternal bond. Now does that mean we are soulmates? Of course not, because we created that love. Our love didn't exist from our first encounter. We had to *breathe* life into our love.'

'That's a beautiful story Aydin.'

'In Turkey we have a saying that goes like this *kalbini kapatma çünkü aklın bir kişiye bağlı*. Which means don't *close* your heart because your mind depends on one person. What I'm trying to say Chuck is open your heart to let others in and see how quickly your mind will follow. Now let's get you some food, on the house this time. What do you want?'

'The usual I guess.'

'One mix grill coming up.'

He stood up and walked back towards the kitchen. I took up my phone, went through my contacts and called Sade.

6

Sade had visited me on a couple occasions. It was *okay*.

We fucked, ate and talked. I would take her to

Cappadocia, and she would sit by the bench at the park

and watch me skate. There were no arguments and yet

it wasn't *perfect*...I don't know what it was, but I

struggled to feel anything for her. I tried. I really did.

But it just wasn't working. She seemed more like a fan

that was backstage with her favorite artist than a

woman that was trying to impress a man she liked. She

wanted to know too much about me and said too *little*

about herself. I found it boring. I found her boring.

Her boredom made me look at her different. She

wasn't as beautiful as she was when I first saw her at

the poetry reading and her presence didn't get my cock

hard as much as it did the first night we spent together

at my old apartment. I found the little stuff irritating too like the way should pronounce here as *hiya* and how she would call me daddy in bed. It made me uncomfortable to the point where I couldn't cum. I would continue fucking, but my spirit wouldn't be in it. That's the worst type of sex. The type that feels like an obligation...like a 9-5 job you dread going to...like law school. And yet I kept trying. I kept telling myself that next time it would be different, or that if I tried seeing her enough times, I could trick my heart and mind into liking her. So, I did. I continued inviting her over hoping that it would change.

It was Saturday which meant that if was my day off from work. I checked my phone and saw that I had four missed calls from Sade. I called her back.

'Hello.'

'Hey Chuck, it's me. I'm outside.'

'Cool. Coming down now.'

The first two times she came I picked her up from the underground station. I didn't mind. It was only a fifteen-minute bus ride away and I liked the *peacefulness* of sitting on the bus staring out the window. It felt as if my life was in slow motion whiles everybody else around me continued moving. People walking up and down, cars driving past us, construction work being done, the sound of police and ambulance sirens echoing throughout the city. Everybody else was existing whiles I was just *spectating*. I don't know what happened but that day I didn't feel like picking her up. I asked her if she knew the way to the apartment and she said yes. When I woke up on that Saturday, I didn't feel sad, angry, horny or happy, I just felt *empty*. Walking down the stairs to open the door I got a weird feeling…the feeling of wanting to escape. I don't know if I wanted to escape this day, Sade or the thought of Célia that was still lingering in my heart. I just knew I wanted to be alone, and yet here I was attempting to fuck my loneliness away. When I opened the door, it felt as if I was clocking in to start my shift. I felt tired and mentally drained as I took a deep breath and pushed open the door to see her standing there. She didn't have no make-up on as she stood there in her white flare sweatpants a matching white hoodie navy-blue backpack and her hair that was tied in a bun. I couldn't explain it to myself, but she looked *different*. She gave me a kiss and started asking me questions. I was already looking forward to being alone again. I ordered us a large peperoni pizza that we ate in silence on the bed whiles watching a movie she liked. The movie was okay. It was about a class of delinquent teenagers and a newly appointed teacher and her journey to get the students love and approval. We finished the movie and the pizza, and I went into the kitchen to throw away the empty box and came back into the room. I sat on the bed and picked up my phone. It was 9.45pm. I opened up my laptop and tried writing, but even that proved to be difficult as she laid close to me and hovered over the screen asking me questions about the characters and the plot of the novel. After attempting to answer seven of her questions I closed the laptop without writing a single line, went into the fridge cracked open a beer put on my jacket and went outside for a smoke. I stomped the cigarette and stood outside some more before I went in again. I entered the room and saw her on the floor reading The Color Purple by Alice Walker. I liked her taste in books. Too bad I couldn't like her. She saw me entering closed the book and faced me.

'Where did you go?'

'Outside.'

'What did you do?'

'Smoke.'

'Cool. How was it outside?'

'Okay, I guess. Look do you want to watch a movie?'

'Sure. What movie?'

'What movie do you want to watch?'

'I don't know. You pick. Anything is fine with me.'

We watched one and a half movies I had seen before. I had to end the second one halfway through because I had enough of her questions. I thought maybe sex would tire her out. We kissed, but something was *missing*...we fucked, but it was no longer *exciting*...I felt as if we were married. I like cuddles but that night I just kissed her on the forehead turned around and went to sleep. The next morning, I woke up before her and again I felt empty. I went to the fridge cracked open a beer and took it with me in the shower. I stood in the shower drinking and wondering where it all went wrong. How I couldn't feel anything for a woman I once thought I would feel everything for. I stared down at my cock and started feeling anger and betrayal. It fooled me again. I had managed to fuck myself into a situation I no longer wanted to be in, and most likely end up hurting a woman that didn't deserve that hurt. I was an anarchist that believed that no man should be controlled by governments, rules, institutions, and other humans and yet here I was being controlled by my little [medium] cock. An ugly cock for that. A cock that just wanted to create chaos and heartbreak. A cock that didn't have any regard for other people's emotions or feelings. A cock that was the opposite of my soul. I didn't have much left of my soul, but the little I had was caring, loving and kind. I wanted to chop off my cock and keep my soul, but who was I fooling. The feeling of a wet cunt *triumphs* that of kindness. I got out of the shower looked at myself in the mirror and finished the rest of my beer before I went back into the room. I entered the room and saw her sitting on the bed talking on the phone. She saw me entering and ended the phone call. Fuck. I could feel her eyes staring at me as I made my way towards my closet with the towel wrapped around my waist. She waited until I got dressed before speaking.

'Chuck, you were gone a long time. Are you okay?'

'No. Not really.'

'What's wrong?'

'This.'

'What about this?'

'Does this feel right to you, Sade?'

'Do you mean like me and you?'

'For Christ sakes yes! What is it with you and asking all these goddamn questions?!'

I could see on her face that a mixture of sadness and confusion was clouding her mind. 'I'M FUCKING SORRY CHUCK!!...I just wanted to spend time with you and be with you since I like you...but I'll leave I don't want to stay where I'm not wanted...'

She stood up from the bed and started reaching for her backpack that was on the ground near my skateboard and her sneakers. 'Relax Sade. It's not that *bad*.'

'Is it good?'

'It depends. Do you want the painful *truth* or a *pleasant* lie?'

'YOU KNOW WHAT FUCK YOU CHUCK!! I'M FUCKING LEAVING! YOU'RE SUCH A MISERABLE PIEACE OF SHIT!!!'

'Okay...I understand.'

'THAT'S JUST IT I DON'T THINK YOU ACTUALLY UNDERSTAND WHAT THE FUCK YOU'RE DOING!!

You meet a girl that was perfectly happy being single and you start telling her how much you like her, how being in her presence makes you forget your sadness and how you could see a future with her. You make people fall in love with you and then when you're done with them you just throw them to the side like they didn't mean anything...You're fucking with people's life and emotions...the funniest thing is that you make yourself out to be different from most men when you're just the same...matter of fact you're actually worse. At least they're honest about their evil *intentions*. Whiles you hide yours behind sadness and slick words...You're the worst kind Chuck.'

I sat on the bed as I watched her put her sneakers on and make her way towards the door. 'You're right Sade...I'm sorry...I understand.'

She turned around towards me.

132

'The saddest part about all this is that you had a good thing going and yet you decided to *self-sabotage* it...I don't know what you're looking for Chuck, but I hope you find it.'

'Thank you. Text me when you're home.'

'FUCK YOU!!'

She slammed the door behind her, and I laid down on my bed. I had looked forward to being alone, but now I didn't know if I wanted to be alone. I don't know what I felt when I laid on my bed, but I knew it wasn't a good feeling. It was a mixture of emptiness and self-hatred. The worst kind. The same way how Sade told me that I was the worst kind of man. Deep down I knew she was right. I was the worst child, lover...human being. Usually, I would blame the lack of love in my childhood but as a twenty-two-year-old man I no longer had any excuses for being the way I was. I don't know what's wrong with me or why I'm like this. *Tears* started running down my eyes. Now I felt pain and self-hatred. I didn't like hurting people and yet I pushed away everybody that tried loving me. WHAT THE FUCK IS WRONG WITH ME. I struggled to love myself and I could never figure out how to love someone else. Sade was someone that cared for me, wanted to spend time with me and yet I chose to push her away. The same way I pushed Célia, my grandmother, my mother and everyone else away. I started crying again. I felt alone, vulnerable, naked. I wanted to be held, and yet I had no one to hold me. OH, CHARLES YOU SAD UGLY FUCK!! Is death the only thing that befits this blackhole I call soul? Do I have a soul? Would a man with a soul hurt those he cares for? I spent my life drowning my sorrow in alcohol and my nights reminiscing about how I lost it all. A broken soul in a young body that was a stranger to the feeling of having anybody. In this pathetic pursuit for happiness, it seems like I only encounter sadness. My desperate lifelong search for a love that I thought would fill the *void* in my life made me question whether alcohol would be my only wife.

I heard a knock at the door raised my head and saw Adrian standing by the entrance. He came over and sat on the edge of the bed.

'I just saw Sade storm out the apartment. What was that about?'

'She got tired I guess...'

'What, did you two argue or something?'

'Maybe...no not really. She just realized that sometimes there's a *thin* line between love and hate.'

'You and your fucking girls' man. You know sometimes I envy you Chuck...your freedom... the girls you have coming in and out the apartment... But then I see you when you're alone and that enviousness fades away and is replaced with pity. You're a complicated man Chuck. You live a life that most men would envy, but a loneliness that most people would pity…'

'It's frustrating Adrìan. My cock is an extrovert, but my heart is recluse…the best writers tend to live a lonely life, so I don't know if my loneliness is a curse or a blessing…I'll ask the Gods when I die. Anyways, how are things between you and Esther?'

'It's okay…well I mean I love her but sometimes I feel *suffocated* by our relationship.'

'You want to leave her?'

'No. I think I just want the chance to *miss* her. We sleep, wake up, eat, and do everything together. It's like she's always fucking there. I don't know man…in a way it makes me miss being single…'

'It's ironic how fragile the human heart is when it comes to love. Too little of it makes us angry and too much of it gets us annoyed. In a way it makes you wonder if love was meant for us at all...when we don't have it, we long for it and when we have it, we don't know what to do with it.'

'So, what do you think I should do?'

'If I knew the answer to that question my dear friend, Sade would be naked in my bed right now.'

He left the room and I laid back down.

I woke up checked my phone and saw that it was 11.26pm. For some reason I woke up too *restless* to not do nothing and too *lazy* to do anything. In the end I decided to put on my denim jacket and go out for a walk. The cool August breeze made it refreshing to be outside. The road towards the park that was a couple of blocks away from the apartment was busy that night. The chicken shops were open, the line to get into the clubs were starting to get packed and all around me people were busy talking. I walked in silence feeling like a spectator again amidst the workers, loners, lovers and troublemakers. I walked into a corner shop bought a bottle of white wine and a pack of cigarettes before I continued my journey. I reached the park and sat on one of the benches that was in the open space opened up the wine and lit a cigarette. The dark sky was clouded with stars and the midnight moon hovered over the buildings that surrounded the park. The more I drank the more I kept thinking about God. As someone that never believed in religion, I now found myself envious of those who did. My grandmother tried making me into a believer, but I guess some souls weren't meant to be saved. Religion found those who felt *lost* the same way how a prostitute would develop a knack to spot those who were willing to pay for pussy. And yet here I sat, too broken to be *saved* and too poor to be fucked. I started contemplating what life I'm living, and if my life was worthy enough to be saved by

God even if it's filled with *sin*. Is it too late for me to secure a place in heaven or will God send me to hell to teach me a lesson? How do I keep smiling when my heart is slowly shattering? How can I keep a pure soul when I can feel it breaking?

I took a sip. One more sip. More sips. Before I knew it, the bottle was empty. We all have an escape mechanism from the cruelties of this world. Shopping, golf, jogging, fashion, working, training, drawing, drugs, God. However way you look at it, we all have an outlet we seek when the going gets tough and times get rough. For me it was alcohol. I could no longer differentiate the taste. I only drank it for the effect. It gave me the extra boost I needed in my desperate attempt to run away from my mind. I opened the pack and lit another cigarette oblivious to the fact that I was no longer alone. She just stood there watching me in her tight black leather dress and black ankle boots. I don't know if she was going to rob, kill or fuck me. You could never tell with women. I had met many of them during my lifetime, but each one was different. They fucked different. Kissed different. And loved different. I think that's why I was *addicted* to them. Men were dull and predictable. Sort of like fairytales. Yes, every story was different, but the endings were all the same. But women, wow. They were all ticking *timebombs* that could be triggered by the slightest of emotion. Emotions they themselves couldn't control. See, women spent their whole life trying to know themselves whiles us men spent our life trying to understand them. We were doomed from the beginning. We could never understand women and yet our hearts would always *crave* one. Think of all the tragic love stories and the mans ill-fated demise caused by love. Romeo and Juliet... Anthony and Cleopatra... Othello and Desdemona...Love does not treat us men fairly. We are addicted to it, and it misuses our addiction. It makes us work for it, long for it, pay for it, kill for it, go to war for it. And then when we have it, it blinds us from seeing the destruction it causes in our lives. Love is a silent killer that preys on the *weak*…The men…Me.

She stretched out her hand. 'Can I have a cigarette?'. I nodded my head in silence and handed her the cigarette pack together with the lighter. She picked up a cigarette and put it in-between her plump lips that were covered in berry red lipstick. We continued smoking in silence. She had a dark complexion with a slim face and black dreadlocks that reached down to her spine. She looked like the type that belonged backstage at a rock concert with the lead singer instead of an empty park with a man that was drinking his sorrows away. I wondered if God felt bad for me and sent her down to breathe *life* into my dead soul. She flicked the cigarette sat down next to me and crossed her legs. The way her hands were stroking her legs turned me on. She stared at me with her black almond shaped eyes before she finally spoke.

'You look like shit.'

'I feel worse.'

'It's that why you're sitting here drinking alone?'

'No. That's because I don't care for people...parties or socializing. I'm a loner, a good one at that.'

'What else do you do aside from being lonely?'

'I write...well I used to. I haven't written anything lately. It might be God punishing me.'

'What are you being punished for?'

'*Sinning*. I'm a sinner baby, that's all I do. You should leave. I've heard bad luck is contagious.'

'I'll take my chances. What do you write about?'

'Everything and anything I guess...heartbreak...sadness...See I have a toxic relationship with love and now it's made me it's enemy. So, I spend my days writing about it, hoping that it will give me a second chance ...'

'A writer that argues with love, and yet lives in the *city* of love. Isn't that a recipe for bad love?'

'Has love ever been good? It finds us, wines and dines us, fucks us and then leaves us. We spend our lives chasing love whiles it runs away from us.'

'That's why you have to *enjoy* it. When we have it, we spend so much time thinking, fearing and planning it that we forget to live it.'

'Have you ever had it?'

'Not yet...I've come close, but it always died.'

'What killed it`'

'My *mind*.'

We sat in silence again, but this time it was different. It felt comfortable. I put my hand on her leg and she turned towards me. She looked at me up and down before she kissed me. I still wanted to talk, but I liked kissing more. You could make someone fall in love with just a *kiss*, but a stranger would still be a stranger after sex. Kissing is personal and intimate. My girlfriend could fuck any man, but her kissing someone else would shatter me and turn me into a madman. Every kiss with a woman was different, and this one was up there. Only person I could think of that could compare to this was Célia. I thought about where she was tonight. Probably wrapping her mouth around Matisse's cock. A rush of anger overcame me, and I kissed her *harder*. She sat on top of me as I pressed her lips onto mine. She removed her lips and smiled as she looked into my eyes. It felt intense. I felt alive. I stared back wrapped my hand around her hair and pressed her face against mine. I'm sorry God, my soul longs for heaven but my cock belongs in hell.

It was hard to do anything with the dress she had on.

'Let's go back to mine.'

She stood up looked at me and laughed. 'Wow you're really fast huhh.'

'What do you mean?'

'I don't even know your name, but you want me to come back to yours.'

'Chuck.'

'What?'

'My name. It's Chuck. What's yours?

'Jhené.'

'I like that name. Should we go back to mine?'

She took a hold of my hand smiled and gave me a kiss, 'Okay Chuck.'

'What made you paint this?'

She was pointing at one of my paintings that was hanging on the wall. It was a white canvas filled with words describing different emotions, question marks and symbols. I stood up from the bed and walked up behind her.

'Sadness and alcohol.'

'I like it. I like how everything is smudged together to give it a rugged look. What is the painting supposed to mean?'

'I don't know. My mind I guess...how my mind is filled with thoughts my tongue can't express.'

'Thoughts my tongue can't express. Huh...I like that. Which of the emotions are you feeling now?'

I put one hand around her waist and used the one that was free to point towards the word that was painted in green. 'Happy I think...'

She turned around and gazed into my eyes. 'Why do you feel happy?'

'I don't know...I think it's you. You're refreshing and different...in a good way. And good is not a word I use often to describe my life.'

She smiled, 'You're good with words Chuck...I must give you that.'

'The curse of being a sinful writer...'

I put my hand on her face and drew her close to mine. We moved over to the bed as I laid on top of her and was kissing her all over. Forehead. Mouth. Neck. Leg. I spread her legs apart and saw her black lace underwear. I slid her panties to the side and went to work. Finger in and out and tongue rolling up, down and around. I could feel her legs vibrate whiles she was gripping the bedsheet. I enjoyed it. Hearing her moan and curse and feeling every little body movement she made. I don't know how long I was down there, but it was long enough. I came back up.

'Take off your dress.'

'Okay but no sex.'

'Why not?'

'I don't know…I don't want this to just be another meaningless hook up…I like talking to you. Being around you. I want to get to know you. But if you don't feel the same way it's okay. I'll just leave…'

'No that's fine I like this. What do you want to do?'

'I don't know. Can you just come and hold me?'

'Okay.'

My heart was smiling but my cock was angry. I liked it. Was this God giving me another chance at regaining my soul? I held her in my arms as we continued talking and kissing. We spoke about past lovers, childhood traumas, music, fears, past experiences and future expectations. Laying behind her and feeling the warmth from her naked body I started feeling something. I don't know what it was...but I was looking forward to finding out.

7

A week had gone by and I hadn't heard anything from Jhené. I tried everything. Calling. Texting. And received nothing back. I kept replaying the night we spent together in my head, thinking about if I said or did something wrong. Was I dull?... Did I talk too much?... Did I not listen enough?... Was I not her type?... Should I have asked more questions?

Every attempt at moving on was spoiled by the thought of her reappearing in my mind. Whenever she crossed my mind, I would distract myself by writing. I wrote between ten to fifteen pages every night. I didn't drink as much that week and I wasn't feeling sad, and yet I wrote *well*. It felt strange. I wrote with passion, emotion and a sense of rawness. Like a sailor writing to a lover, he hasn't seen for months. I continued calling but she didn't pick up. In the end I tried convincing myself that it was over, and yet my heart didn't want me to stop. I longed for her touch, voice, laughter, smile, sassiness. I longed for her...

The online blog where I published my poetry was starting to gain attraction after a public figure shared one of my poems on her social media account and the owner of Le Syndicat called me that same week asking if I could perform at the bar on Saturday. I would receive 280 euros to read for thirty minutes and a driver that would take me to the location. I had mix feelings when it came to reading poetry. Standing on that stage alone with everyone's eyes on you as you read them your most personal thoughts and insecurities, you felt vulnerable and *exposed*. I experienced nausea before every reading, which I cured with alcohol. Too little would made me overthink and too much would make me sloppy. Anybody could write a poem but reading it was different. You had to maintain their attention whiles at the same time make them feel every word and emotion. You had all kind of crowds. Old, calm, young, reckless, rowdy, talkative, silent. You had to understand and *adjust* to the crowd and make them respect you. Le Syndicat was a known bar in the tourist part of city. Looking at it from the from the street it didn't have the appearance of a regular bar, as the front was covered in colorful decorations, graffiti and posters. Entering the bar yellow curtains were draped over walls covered in marker drawn pictures and written messages. The lounge was dark, mostly lit up by candles on the tables and the streetlights. Old school hip hop was playing in the background which added a throwback touch to the atmosphere in the bar. There were a few tables along the wall as you walked in, a few seats at the bar and a lounge seating in the back.

Upon entering the bar, I was met by Julien Fontaine who was the owner of the place. He looked like the typical young night club owner, in his light blue denim jeans, black tee and greasy slick backed hair that had a dark brown color in it.

'Are you Charles Johnson?'

'Yes. I'm him.'

'I've read a couple of your poems man. You're talented. Honestly can't wait to hear you read tonight.'

'Thank you.'

'Do you know when you're going on?'

'I was told 9.30.'

'That's right. Anyways I have to go now, but just make yourself at home. Is there anything you need?'

'Beer. A lot of it.'

'Try our cocktails man. Trust me you won't regret it. Have as many of them as you want, it's on the house.'

'Thank you.'

He left and I made my way towards the bar. I ordered a piña colada which consisted of white rum, coconut cream and pineapple juice. I sat and glanced around the bar that was starting to get crowded. There was a different blend of hip people with the men dressed in

Stan Smith sneakers, jeans and scruffy beards and the women having serious red lips and just-woke-up hair. I checked my phone it was 9.15pm. I ordered two more piña coladas.

I got introduced by a woman with a skinny figure and short blond hair. I read old poems and new poems. After the second poem we started feeling at ease with each other. I talked in-between the reading feeding of their positive energy. They took a liking to the poems about mental health and the complicated transition from teenage hood to adulthood and how we spent our time reminiscing about our younger and better days. I chose to end the reading with a poem titled *broken*.

She kept wondering how it could all go so wrong

A love story turned into a sad song

Desperately trying to move on

Forcing herself to accept the fact that

His love for her is gone

But it's hard

When the love fades away

And yet the memories stay

Or even when the relationship is a distant memory

Will she ever

Get over the pain and agony

He caused

A queen now doubting her self-worth

Looking in the mirror

No longer able to recognize herself

Because without him

She struggles to find completeness

Love is a language a woman speaks fluently

With each word rolling off her tongue beautifully

But with just one kiss

A man can numb her mind

To the point where she forgets that

In this life

You can never call someone forever mine

I finished got off stage and walked with Julien to the lounge in the back. He was carrying two vodka martinis, handed me one and sat across from me.

'Wow. That was great Charles. How do you do it? How do you manage to captivate and silence a chatty audience like that?'

'It's in the eyes. The mouth and body can *lie*, but the eyes...the eyes have an uncanny way of always telling the truth. Look them in the eyes and make them feel every emotion you're feeling.'

'I'll remember that next time I suspect my girlfriend of cheating.'

'Love is not treating you well?'

'Man, it's these fucking girls. They don't care about nothing besides money and fame. They don't care about who you are, only what you can do for them. She parties everyday surrounding herself around men I don't know and whenever I bring it up, she tells me I party just as much. I don't party I run bars and clubs. That's my job...'

'Love can be a cruel bitch sometimes.'

'Tell me about it. Don't fall for it Charles. Love is a burdensome *trap* that uses women as its bait. Us men give it our all and receive nothing but *headache* back...'

'I'll remember that Julien.'

'Anyways back to business. I would like you to read here two to three times a month. You'll get 300 euros after each reading.'

'I'll think about it.'

'Do that. You have my number. Text or call me when you've made a decision. They love you here Charles. Also, I have someone I want you to meet.'

'Who?'

'His name is Larry Walker. He's an American literary agent that's based here in Paris.'

'Okay.'

Julien left and came back with Larry. He was a baldheaded dark man in his forty's that was wearing a black blazer, white tee and dark blue washed jeans. Julien introduced us to each other before he left again. Larry reached out and shook my hand. He sat down next to me.

'You're a talented poet Charles. Have you thought about publishing anything?'

'I have.'

'What?'

'A novel and a collection of poems.'

'That's great. How's the novel coming along?'

'It's okay. I'm halfway there.'

'What is the novel about?'

'It's about three delinquent teenagers living in a society they struggle to fit in and a city they can never seem to call home.'

'That's similar to how I felt being raised in North Carolina until I moved to Germany to study. I've now lived in France for twenty years, but it wasn't until five years ago I started calling this place home.'

'What changed?'

'I met and married the love of my life.'

'How long did you two know each other before your marriage?'

'We married two months after our first date.'

'Isn't that too soon?'

'No, not really. Love is a sensation you cannot control and when it hits you it hits you strong. Your body starts overflowing with emotions and you feel inseparable from that person. Love doesn't require you to have known someone for a long time, or even know them at all. Love is not based on time or *logic*. Some of my friends called me crazy for wanting to marry someone after knowing them for two months. But I wasn't crazy at all...I was just a man in love...'

I listened closely whiles nodding my head. I liked Larry. More than I liked Julien. Men like Julien looked at love as a contract that comes with its terms and conditions instead of an experience that must be felt. They saw love as a means to fulfill their needs. They tried to define, label and put instructions on love. Without knowing that love has no limits and cannot be governed or restricted by the rules of this earth.

'How do you know when you're in love?'

He hesitated before he looked at me and replied. 'I think it's when you become addicted to their presence.

Seek their presence. Have a constant crave for their presence. And when you feel the need to tell them I love you whenever you're around them, touch them or miss them. Are you in love?'

'I don't know...I think so.'

'If you feel it, go after it. Love is hard to find and easy to lose...Anyways, enough about love. Let's talk business. I've been in the book industry for fifteen years now Charles and take great pride in finding up and coming writers and turn them into household names. I have the network needed to get you out there and you have the talent it takes to make it.

'What will you do?'

'I'll represent you. Get you bookings, publishing deals. I'll do everything. You just have to continue writing and reading as well as you did tonight. Not many poets can do what you just did on that stage. The way you transferred your energy and emotions to the audience and how you made them feel every word you spoke. That's a talent you don't come across every day. So, what do you think?'

'Sounds good. What do you need?'

'I'll give you my number. Just email me your poetry and a synopsis of the novel. I'll text you my email address.'

We got the formalities out of the way before Julien appeared again standing in front of us.

'You men want anything to drink?'

Larry stood up and shook his hand. 'Not for me. I'll be going. Too old for this shit. Charles, it was nice meeting you and I'm looking forward to working with you. Julien, as always thank you for your hospitality.'

'Thanks for coming Larry. What about you Charles, anything you'd like?'

I looked up at him. 'Can I have another vodka martini?'

'Sure. I'll tell one of the bartenders to bring it.'

He left and I was alone in the lounge. I never cared for clubs and bars. Too crowded and the music was too loud. I preferred to drink alone or in the company of woman. We all drink for something. To celebrate...to be happy...to be social...to be confident...to be sexual...to be wild. Whiles I drank to feel *nothing*.

I saw a figure walk towards the lounge with a glass in their hand. Jhené. She had on black bootcut jeans and a white Metallica tee. I stood up gave her a hug and we both sat down.

She took a hold of my hand. 'You never told me you wrote poetry. I watched your whole performance. It was beautiful. You have a soothing voice.'

I released my hand from hers. 'Thank you.'

'Chuck… What's wrong?'

'What are you even doing here?'

'I work here. Why are you acting like this?'

'Like what?'

'Like you don't want to speak to me.'

'Are you serious?? I've tried calling and texting you.'

'Chuck you don't understand. I can explain…'

'Explain what?'

'Why I haven't replied back.'

'Okay.'

'Remember that night we met at the park when you asked me about what killed my attempts at love, and I said my mind?'

'Yes?'

'I'm *bipolar* Chuck. That's what I meant with my mind. There are days, weeks even months where I feel too depressed, sad and drained to talk to or be around people. This week was one of those.'

'Why didn't you tell me?'

'Because I didn't want to *scare* you away. I don't know...I liked the night we had...I like you. Most people can't handle or understand someone like me...'

'I'm not most people. In fact, I hate people...but I like you.'

She smiled leaned over and gave me a peck. 'That last poem you read was it about someone?'

'Yes.'

'Who?'

'A love long *gone.*'

'Stand up. Let's dance.'

'No thank you. I'm okay right here.'

'Aww please Chuck. Do it for me…'

I'm a sucker for pretty faces and attractive eyes and she had *both*. Drowning in the music dancing skin to skin. My hands on her waist and our eyes locked in. Her smile had me blushing as I felt my heart thumping. Should I kiss her? Or should I wait? This the type of dilemma I hate… Or maybe it was just fate that our souls were supposed to meet? Was tonight the night I felt an angel's tender lips? I held her face with my hands drew her close and gave her a long and passionate kiss.

Thirty minutes later her shift was over, and we were in a cab heading back to my apartment. She threw her red leather jacket on the ground and jumped on the bed. 'I hate that job so much. Can't wait to quit!'

I walked over and laid next to her as we were both staring up at the roof. 'I spoke with your boss today.'

'Who? Julien?'

'Yes.'

'What did he say?'

'Nothing much. He just wanted me to perform at the bar on a regular basis.'

'Are you going to do it?'

'I don't know yet. He told me to think about it. What do you think about him?'

'He's such a misogynistic fuck. Always complaining about his girlfriend cheating on him and yet he flirts with every woman at work.'

'Did he flirt with you too?'

She turned on her side and looked at me. 'He knows better than to try that shit with me. I would've handed him a slap and a lawsuit...And why do you ask, would that have made you *jealous*?'

'I'm a man without emotions, Jhené. That's how my soul has managed to be alive for this long. Caring is for the weak and living. I'm just dead and existing.'

'Too bad you can't lie as good as you read... Ouuu can you read a poem for me now?'

'Next time baby. Let's go to bed.'

We both started undressing until we were back in bed only covered in our underwear. This time again she told me no sex. She didn't feel like she knew me well enough. And to be honest it didn't bother me. As previously mentioned, I'm a *junkie* for kissing. I laid on top of her as I kissed her viscously whiles choking her. She reached down pulled out my cock and was stroking it up and down her panties. I slid her panties to the side, and she continued the stroking motion on her hairless cunt. Up. Down. Up. Down. I was waiting for her to put it in. After the painful realization started sinking into my mind, I chose to please her in other ways. I was rubbing her clit switching between the index and middle finger. She started moaning and I continued rubbing whiles kissing her like a lunatic. The moaning became louder. I was getting harder and harder. I slid a finger into her wet cunt and shaped it into a hook. Fast. Slow. Fast. Slow. Fast. I went down on her and continued the rubbing motion with my tongue.

'Chuck...ahhh...don't stop...FUCCckkk don't stop...AHHHHhhh...come up come up I want to suck your cock.'

We switched positions as I laid down and took my boxers off. She put both her hands around my cock spat on it and wrapped her mouth around it. She continued sucking whiles her hands were going up and down the cock in a twisting motion. I could feel my toes twitching and my legs raising.

'AHH FUUUckkkk don't stop...FUCKK YESSS BABYY DON'T YOU FUCKING STOOOOoooppp.'

I grabbed her head shoved it down on my cock and made her gag on it. 'AHHH FUCKKK JHENÉ I'MM CUUuuminggggg.'

I *exploded* in her mouth. She swallowed the cum stood up and walked to the bathroom.

The next time I saw Jhené was the 1st of november. It was her birthday and I promised her I would make us dinner. I took the bus from Mairie de Saint Ouen to Barbés-Rochechouar and from there embarked on a seven-minute walk before reaching the organic market at Marché Anvers. I lost track of time at the market walking cluelessly around searching for the ingredients needed to make alfredo shrimp. I boarded the bus towards Gare Montparnasse with a plastic bag full of groceries. Fettuccini pasta, heavy cream, parmesan cheese, shrimp, garlic, white wine and parsley. Jhené lived in the South Pigalle area of Paris which meant that I had to get off at Blanche and from there walk to her apartment. Her apartment was located on a crowded street packed with shops, restaurants and cafés with tall beige apartment buildings filling up the empty spaces on the sidewalk. I called her. Ring...ring...ring...

'Hi Chuck, are you outside?'

'I think so, what's the number on the building? All the apartments here look the same.'

'It's number 5. Where are you?'

'Okay. Cool. I'm standing outside building number 5.'

'Cool. Just ring the intercom and I'll open the door for you. Then you just take the elevator up to the fourth floor. My apartment number is 377.'

'Okay.'

Jhené lived in a four-bedroom apartment which she shared with other people. Walking into the apartment it was a mixture of tidiness and cleanliness. The hallway had shoes that were spread across the ground. The kitchen had a couple of plates and pans in the sink but other than that was relatively tidy. There were two drying racks in the living room near the black couch, a black and white framed picture of the Brooklyn bridge that was hung above the TV stand that had a medium sized bookshelf next to it. I put my arms around her and gave her an enthusiastic kiss.

'Happy birthday baby...'

'Thank you. Do you need help with the food?'

'No. Don't worry. Just sit down and let me do the cooking.'

'Okay. I'm glad you here, you know. I've missed you.'

'I've missed you too Jhené.'

I sat the plastic bag on the kitchen counter and took out the ingredients. I boiled the pasta simmered the ingredients needed for the sauce cooked the shrimp on a hot pan until they were pink and opaque before I tossed the shrimp and pasta together with the creamy sauce. She got rid of the magazines and laptop that were on their wooden kitchen table before I served the food. She opened the bottle of white wine and brought out two wine glasses.

'Where are your roommates?'

'Uhmm Christina is in her room, Anais went back home to Toulouse for the weekend and Marine is staying over at her boyfriend's place.'

'Okay. Sit down let's eat. Tell me how it tastes.'

She picked up a fork and took a bite.

'Oh my God Chuck this is good. I've never had a man cook for me before.'

'Not even your dad?'

'He was never in my life to be honest. He left us when I was six. I have a stepdad, but he doesn't do much either. He just goes to work comes homes and lays on the couch all day watching football, leaving my mom to cook and clean. I don't know, there are days when I just hate men...'

'Do you?'

'Yes. Well except you. I can't explain it, but you're just different. You're not like most men out there.'

'According to *some* women I'm worse.'

'How so?'

'I don't know. I think we're all angels or *demons* depending on who you ask.'

'So, what do you think you are?'

'I have no clue. I'll let you know when I find out.'

'Good. I'm glad that you came though…I don't really care about birthdays, but I like this one…'

We finished our food took our glasses and went out on the balcony. I check my phone it was 11.30pm and yet the street was still lively with people walking up and down, cars honking and loud music echoing throughout the area. There's a thin line between confidence and arrogance and people who played loud music were guilty of crossing that line. Forcing you to listen to their heinous taste turning the volume up to the point where you could no longer ignore it. There was a lot about Paris that made it a beautiful city, but

Parisians arrogance when it came to their music wasn't one of them.

'I read the chapters you emailed me. And honestly Chuck I loved them. You made the characters and the story feel real. Christina and I sat up the whole night reading and talking about it whiles drinking wine. She loved it too. She said your style of writing reminds her a lot of Hemingway in A Moveable Feast. I'm in awe of your talent Chuck...'

'Thank you. I like that you *care*.'

'Have you chosen a title yet?'

'Yes. Rebels without a cause...'

'What does that mean?'

'People who are dissatisfied with the society they live in but do not have a specific reason to fight for.'

'That's beautiful. It fits the story...other than that, how are you? You okay?'

'I don't know. I feel like I'm just *here* you know. Like I'm cruising and not really living. Almost like this earth is my prison and dying is my release date and my ticket to *freedom*.'

'I turned twenty-four today and I feel like that's how life is for those our age. I spend my days reminiscing about the times I could call myself a teen, asking myself if this is how I thought my life would turn out, struggling in my early twenties trying to sort it out. Going through hidden battles with depression, confusion and anger as I often think about how my childhood best friend became a stranger...'

'Don't you find it ironic how we live in a generation that's allergic to showing emotion, and yet deep down we all feel the same way...lost and empty.'

'It is. We walk around with masks on as we try to live a picture-perfect life on social media when the truth is that none of us know what the fuck we are doing. We act like we have it all together when the reality is that mentally we're all slowly breaking down and yet we are too prideful to admit it to each other...'

'A generation of lust that doesn't understand the concept love living in a world filled with sorrow and where we misuse drugs to escape the fears of tomorrow.'

'Speaking of lust, do you want to see the clothes I bought today? I have a feeling you might like it.'

'Sure baby, it's your special day after all.'

She walked me into her bedroom that was lit up in red led lighting. There were paintings hung up on the wall above her desk, a wall that was covered in photos of her friends and loved ones, a sliding mirror closet and a low modern queen-sized bed that was next to two large casement windows that looked out towards the street and a supermarket. I sat on the bed as she undressed. One by one she tried on every outfit and modeled it for me. First it was a red leather dress that revealed her hourglass shape, black leather pants that brought attention to her ass and a white silk blouse that gave her a corporate look.

'I'll be right back. The last one is going to take some time to put on.'

'Okay.'

She went to the bathroom and came back five minutes later. 'Chuck! Close your eyes.'

'Okay.'

'Okay. You can open them now.'

She had on a red underwired lace bra matching thong and a red satin gown.

'How do I look?'

'Like a runway model baby...come here...'

'Take off your clothes first...'

I quickly started undressing taking off my denim jeans
and brown tee.

'I said everything Chuck...your socks and boxers too.'

'Okay.'

She put music on and sat on top of my naked body. Her
music taste wasn't bad and her body in that lingerie
wasn't either. I grabbed the back of her head and
pressed it towards my face and kissed her. She
grabbed my cock with one hand slid her panties to the
side with the other and mounted my cock in. She stared
deeply into my eyes and smiled.

'Happy birthday to me...'

I put both hands on her waist as she started riding and bouncing. Back and forth... Up and down... Back and forth... Up and down... Switching between going fast and slow. I looked to the left and saw our reflection in the mirror. It drove me crazy I pulled her bra down enough for her nipples to pop out and started fucking her like a madman. I put both hands on her neck and choked her whiles thrusting viciously.

'AHHHhhh FUUCckkk CHUCK I FUCKING LOVE YOUuuu.'

I stopped and looked at her. 'Wait what did you say?'

'Oh my God this is so awkward...I'm so sorry. I don't know why I said that...'

'No, it's okay. I liked it. Say it again. Shout it louder this time.'

She resumed the motion again. 'I FUCKING LOVE YOUUU CHUCKK!! FUCK ME BABY FUCK MmmeeE.'

We switched positions as she laid on her back and spread her legs. I got on top of her and mounted in my cock. I gave her between ten to fifteen strokes before I felt my cock wanting to explode.

'AHHHhhh I'M ABOUT TO CUMMM AHHH FUCKK.'

'COME IN ME BABYYY COME FOR ME CHUCKkkk'

'ARGGHHHhhh FUUckkkk.'

She pushed me off. 'Chuck, did you just cum in me??!'

I nodded my head whiles wheezing. 'I thought you told me to?'

'Yes. But I didn't think you would actually do it. I'm not on the fucking pill Chuck. Fuck…'

She stood up and flounced out towards the bathroom. I shouted after her. 'HAPPY BIRTHDAY JHENÉ!'

'FUCK YOU CHUCK!!'

8

I quit the job at the library and was now reading poetry
full time. The pay wasn't much but it was enough to
pay my rent and maintain a sustainable living. I didn't
skateboard as much as I used to since my weeks were
now spent travelling across the country doing readings.
Larry and I would either drive, take bus or fly to our
destinations. Sitting in business class with the lawyers,
businessmen, fancy suit wearers and law-abiding
citizens I felt like I was cheating the *system*. A plane
ticket that was prepaid and a man that got paid to read
poems and consume alcohol. I must've been everything
they hated. A fraudulent man that had managed to

infiltrate a place he didn't belong surrounded by people he didn't share any values with. Every flight I could feel them stare deep into my somewhat empty soul as their suspicions about me not being one of them started to sink in. I tried to dress accordingly but even that proved to be unsuccessful. In the end I had to be the most easily recognizable man on the plane. Sitting in my bootcut denim jeans, white converse, white tee, a black blazer with patches on it a trucker cap with my dreadlocks sticking out and a glass of vodka in my hand. I was sitting in the window isle next to Larry headed to Strasbourg for a reading. I had a reading at the University of Strasbourg hosted by the literature department that was taking place from Wednesday to Friday. Larry removed his headphones and turned his face towards me.

'You feel ready?'

'Yes.'

'I got the monthly report back from the publisher. Your novel is performing extremely well. There are even talks that your book could become the country's bestseller.'

'Okay. Cool.'

'What's wrong Chuck? You seem off. Is everything okay?'

'I don't know man, is anything ever okay? Love is a *poison* that kills us slowly and life is a bloodsucking leech that sucks out the joy in everything good that comes our way...'

'Okay so this is clearly about Jhené. What happened?'

'Nothing. Absolutely nothing. And that's the problem. She's having another episode, so I haven't spoken to her for what a month and a half now. I understand her situation, but I don't know, it's draining.'

'I don't know what to tell you son. Communication is a cornerstone of a relationship... Wait, are you two even a couple?'

'Yes...well no...honestly I don't know. We both don't believe in labelling love and we agreed that what's understood doesn't need to be defined. I'm not sure if we're just going with the flow or if we're exclusive. But then how can I be in a relationship with someone I can't speak to whenever I want.'

'Hmm do you love her?'

'I told her I do on multiple occasions so yeah I guess...'

'Does she love you?'

'Yes. Well, I would like to think so considering that she tells me that every time we speak and whenever we're around each other.'

'Does she love you as *much* as you love her?'

'Is there something you want to tell me Larry? Because I don't like where this is heading.'

'Hey man don't attack me. I'm just asking questions here. Basically, what I'm trying to say is that you're what twenty-three years old now. You have your whole life in front of you, don't take everything so serious. Live life for what it is…an *experience*. You can either continue this cat and mouse game with Jhené and chase something that may not be certain, or you can continue living life as the experience it was meant to be.'

'So, what do you think I should do?'

'That's a decision you have to make yourself. Love wouldn't be love without it's trials and tribulations.'

'You would be a shit therapist.'

'The same way how you're a shit lover. Even your girlfriend that's not your girlfriend won't talk to you.'

'Wow you're a sick and coldhearted old man, Larry. Don't make me fire you...'

'Ahh please. Like you could find someone else that would put up with your bullshit. It's me and you forever kid. Get used to it.'

We both laughed and took a sip of our drinks. As usual he was drinking a glass of scotch whiskey. As an avid scotch lover, he had great liking for Johnnie Walker Gold Label, a blend of whiskies from the Speyside and Highland regions of Scotland mixed together to create a smooth whisky full of vanilla and dark fruit. I stared out the window losing myself in my own thoughts. I started thinking about my life and how much had changed. The good. The bad. The lessons. The experiences. And how it all led to this point. A rush of sadness overcame me. Here I was travelling across the country somewhat living a life I've always wanted and yet I had no one to tell it to or *share* it with. Sade had blocked me. Henry was dead. Célia had moved on and Jhené couldn't be reached. Was I doing something wrong?... What's the point of success if your life is still defined by sadness?... Does achieving my dreams come at the cost of my happiness?... As a man that often doubted if he had a consciousness, I now found myself feeling guilty. Not so much of because of what I've done but rather because of who I was...I was a complicated man indeed, but I tried to be as pure as possible. I really tried, and yet I always seemed to fail, either hurting those around me or hurting myself it didn't matter how good everything was going, in the end someone would be hurt. I felt drained as my head started feeling heavy and my body light. I turned to Larry in an attempt to distract myself from my thoughts.

'How long is it until we land?'

'We got two hours left.'

'Fuck...okay. What's going to happen when we land?'

'Remy Garcon is going to pick us up and drive us to the hotel before we head to the university in the evening. And after the reading there will be a private get together.'

'Who is Remy?'

'The president of the student union that's hosting the event. He's a big fan of yours. He asked if you could sign his book.'

'Okay that's fine. Are we doing a book signing event too or?'

'No. Nothing specific is set up. You can sign books if you want but you don't have to.'

'Okay. Cool.'

'Get some sleep kid. You look tired.'

I woke up to Larry tapping and shaking my arm.

'Chuck...Chuck...we're here.'

We got off the plane and made our way towards baggage claim. French women looked their best at airports as they came in different shapes, sizes and faces. Brunettes, blondes, redheads, ebony, white, Asian. They walked with a mixture of arrogance and elegance with their backs straight, core tight, and shoulders back and down but in a relaxed and not forceful way. Their arms swayed slightly as they walked in a fast pace with their hips straight and the movement coming from their legs. Their confidence and style were a turn on and my eyes would wander from one to the other. Even Larry, a man that was crazy for the love of his life couldn't help himself.

'You're an old dirty bastard Larry. You're old enough to be her dad.'

'Hey man, I'm married not blind. What's the point of having sight if we can't appreciate Gods work?'

'I guess you're right. Perverted but right...'

'Remy is calling. I think he's waiting for us outside. Could you grab our luggage's whiles I answer this call?'

I picked up the luggage's and we headed towards the exit. We got out of the airport and saw Remy standing next to his car in the pick-up area dressed in black dress pants, black dress shoes, and a checkered lightweight jacket. His car was a white BMW 1 series with matt black rims and tinted windows. We got the formalities out of the way, stored the luggage's in the boot and started driving to the hotel. He tried catching eye contact with me through the rear-view mirror.

'Charles, did Larry tell you how much I admire your work?'

'Yes, he did. Thank you.'

'When did you start writing poetry?'

'When I was around six or seven.'

'What made you write?'

'I don't know. Anger, I guess. I was a child that was angry at the world that sought *comfort* in words.'

'Even when you talk it sounds poetic. Man, how do you do it?'

Larry started chuckling and looked at us. 'Don't compliment him too much Remy. He's already an arrogant fuck.'

We all shared a laugh before Remy spoke again. 'No but honestly Charles, at such a young age you've written a novel that could arguable end up as a modern classic and a collection of poems that might be some of the best I've ever read. You're a great writer man.'

'I appreciate the kind words, but the biggest mistake a writer can ever make is to consider himself great. My writing is a piece of trash...but it's a *tolerable* piece of trash. The type of trash you don't mind having in the house because it doesn't smell as much as the other's and you're too lazy to take it out...'

'Well do you have any tips for someone that's trying to write a piece of trash?'

'Alcohol. A lot of it. Alcohol makes our hearts say the things our mind won't *allow* us to...Speaking of alcohol is there any at the hotel'

'Yes. Larry emailed me your itinerary. There's a mini fridge in your room filled up with two six-packs of Heineken, one bottle of Smirnoff and two bottles of Prosecco.'

'I like you Remy and call me Chuck.'

'Thank you, Chuck. If it's not too much to ask, could you read a couple of my poems and let me know what you think?'

'Sure. Email it to Larry and I'll read and give any feedback I have.'

We drove for twenty more minutes before reaching our destination. Remy checked us in and followed us up to our rooms on the second floor before leaving. It was a basic but clean hotel, and although the rooms were slightly small, they still gave off a comfortable aura. I walked over to the mini fridge took out a six pack of beer brought out my portable Bluetooth speaker and sat on the bed. I looked at my phone it was 2.50pm. John Mayer was playing from the speaker as I cracked open a beer and started drinking. I was halfway through Who Says (my favorite song from John) and on my third beer when Larry decided to enter my room.

'Chuck. You'll be going on at 8…Remy will pick us up at 6.45 so we can get in a quick sound check before you go on stage.'

'Okay. Cool.'

'You feeling better?'

'Think so. Just tired.'

'Okay. Make sure to not drink too much. You know how sloppy you get.'

'You really know how to kick a man when he's already down huh? But yes, I know. Just going to finish this pack and that's it.'

'Okay. Love you kid. I'll come back later.'

'Love you too.'

He left and I continued drinking. I turned the speaker off and drank in silence until I finished all six beers. I opened my phone went on my recent calls and redialed

Jhené. No answer. I tried again. No answer. I tried one last time. No answer. What the actual fuck. My head started feeling heavy and my mind was filled with thoughts I didn't have the answers to. I laid down shut my eyes and went to bed. Larry came in to wake me up around 6pm. I showered, got dressed drank a glass of Smirnoff and got in the car. I was reading at Lakeside Theatre which I was told would be at max capacity as over two hundred students would show up to listen to me read for an hour and a half. Literature students were always the worst. A bunch of know it all's that thought they were the next Mark Twain or Oscar Wilde. As they sat there judging analyzing and overthinking every word you spoke, pauses you took and movements you made. Maybe if they all showed up drunk reading for them would be less of a bore. I was dreading standing in front of this crowd two days in a row. I made a mental note to myself to tell Remy I would need more beer. That night I read poems about generational dilemma's, the importance of black lives and the harsh realities regarding racism, discrimination and how the system unfairly treats those of color. I finished that night's reading with a poem titled *Conspiracy*.

Our countries made up by a ruler

That was held in the hands of the white man

They shamed our leader

Because he made us realize *yes we can*

This is the tale of the black man

Living in a society that only sees white

A society where they mistreat our queens

And end the life of our teens

And yet when we proclaim that we're not happy

They deem us as a race that's always angry

When we come together and take a stand

Protesting by either kneeling or raising our hand

They view it as an act of aggression

Even though they were the ones that infiltrated our land

Forced our fathers to become slaves

And our mothers to dig their graves

Denied our children the chance to learn about their history

By erasing it from our country's memory

And yet when we proclaim that we're not happy

They deem us as a race that's always angry

The reading finished and we attended the invite only gathering that took place in the main auditorium. I autographed books and got introduced to a couple of people but aside from that I mostly stood in the corner drinking a glass of some tasteless non-alcoholic fruit punch as I watched Larry walking around and networking. We stared at each other from opposite sides of the room. She looked stunning standing there in a green split thigh floral milkmaid dress that showed off her tan skin tone, white low-heeled sandals and my novel in her hand. I walked over and introduced myself.

'Hi, my name is Charles.'

She made a face whiles looking at me up and down.
'What are you doing?'

'What do you mean?? You totally invited me over with your eyes.'

'Why would I want to talk to an author that loves himself so much that he thinks that every woman that reads his book wants to fuck him?'

'If you think I love myself you must be the most *delusional* person on this earth.'

'Ohhh what so now you're filled with self-pity?'

'No. I just practice a lot of self-realization. Did you like the book?'

'I did. Not as much as these hypocrites here, but I did. I especially loved Audrey's character.'

'What about her did you like?'

'I like how she stood up and *rebelled* against the male patriarchy. A lot of women can relate to living in a society or a household where your voice isn't heard, and everybody having a picture of you in their head that you have to live up to or else you'll get shunned or looked down upon. A world where your *gender* decides what you're supposed to be and how you're supposed to act.'

'How about Teddy?'

'I didn't like him at first to be honest.'

'Why not?'

'Because he just seemed so cliché and wannabe. Trying to force himself to be a part of the popular crew. It wasn't until he met Audrey, he started learning the value of loving yourself and your own solitude.'

'So, you're saying that Audrey was the true rebel in the story whiles Teddy and Will were her sidekicks?'

'Well...isn't that usually how it goes? Men just talk, whiles women *act*. A woman can rebel alone, but a man will need a whole entourage.'

'I like that. What's your name?'

'Valeria.'

'Do you write Valeria?'

'I prefer reading. But yes, I do write poetry sometimes.'

'Okay. I apologize if this might sound too direct, but I don't want to be here in this room surrounded by fake love and I got two champagne bottles back at the hotel I don't want to drink alone. Would you mind joining me?'

'Okay Charles. Where is the hotel?'

'Call me Chuck. And it's not too far from here. I'll call a cab for us I just have to talk to my agent first.'

'Okay.'

I decided to insult the art of conversation by walking over and interrupting Larry's. I tapped him on his shoulder, and he turned around to face me.

'Larry, I need to talk to you.'

'Hey man, what's up?'

'I made my choice.'

'About what?'

'If I should continue and experience life or sit and hope for something that may not be *certain*.'

'Okay. What did you choose?'

'I think I'm going to try and live life. I'm going back to the hotel with Valeria.'

'Val who?'

'Valeria. A woman I just met. We're going back to the hotel. Do you want to come?'

'No. I think I'm staying. I'll make Remy drive me back. You want me to ask him to drive you back?'

'No that's fine. I'll just call a cab.'

'Okay. Have fun. Don't wake up too late tomorrow.'

I walked back to Valeria and we made our way towards the exit whiles I called a cab. We sat in the cab talking about our backgrounds. I told her how I was born during the civil war in Sierra Leone and how my mother gave birth to me at our neighbor's house due to the hospitals being overtaken by the opposition, and how we ended up moving to France. She spoke about how she was born in Columbia but was given away to an adoption agency when she was just a baby before she was adopted by her French foster parents when she was three years old. She mentioned in detail her ongoing dilemma between her adoptive parents wanting her to conform to and accept their culture and her wish to explore and be in tune with her origins, and her long-life pursuit of trying to track down her biological mother. I checked my phone before we entered the room. It was 11.15pm. I walked to the fridge took out a bottle of Prosecco and two glasses from the cupboard. She sat on the bed. I filled up both glasses and gave her one. She stood up in front me. I lifted my glass.

'Let's toast.'

'To what?'

'Love and unplanned memories...'

'Are you a believer in true love?'

'I don't know...see I write a lot about love but to be honest I'm a fraud because I don't know anything about it...but I guess in life we all have one or if we're lucky two chances at true love.'

'I don't agree. I think love is what you make it and with whom you make it with...'

'So, what could you make of us?'

'I don't know. I don't even know you.'

'Does love require you to know someone?'

'I don't know...what do you think it requires?'

'*Chemistry...*'

'Do you think we have that?'

'Mhmm maybe...do you?'

'I don't know...how about you kiss me and find out.'

I put our glasses on top of the fridge walked back and lifted by her thigh as I kissed her excitedly. I was lifting her towards the bed until she looked at me.

'Fuck me on the floor.'

I laid the grey blanket on the ground took the duvet and pillows from the bed and shut the lights off. We undressed and got under the duvet. We laid on our side with me behind her. I lifted her right leg up and tried to mount my cock in. It took me multiple attempts before I found the right hole. I knew I shouldn't have mixed beer, champagne and liquor. I started thrusting as I pushed her blonde curls to the side fondly kissing her neck. The faster I went the louder she moaned.

'AAHHhhh FUUUUckkkk THAT FEELS SO FUCKIIIiiing GGGoood.'

'AHHH YEAHH YOU LIKE THAT??'

'SI PAPI SIIIiiii SE SIENTE TAN BIENnn FUCKKkk.'

I didn't understand what she was saying but it sounded sexy. It turned me on even more. I started switching tempos. Fast. Slow. Up. Down. Faster. Harder. Faster. Faster. I gave her ten more strokes before we switched positions and she laid on her stomach whiles I was on top of her back. I spread her legs apart and mounted my cock back in. I started switching tempos again but this time between slow and hard, and fast and aggressive. She kept speaking Spanish. It was driving me crazy. I didn't know if I could last long. Her cunt was wet. Almost too wet. It was as if she had planned for this to happen already from our first encounter. I kept thrusting whiles pulling her body close to me.

'AHHHH FUCKKK I'M ABOUT TO CUMMMMM.'

'I WANT YOUR CUM ON MY FACE PAPI.'

I quickly rose up and she went on her knees in front of me. I was stroking myself whiles fondling her breasts. She was fingering herself and moaning. We maintained eye contact the whole time. I could feel it. The blood was rushing. My cock wanted to explode. I aimed my cock at her face and watched the cum burst all over her slim beautiful face.

'AHHH FUCKKK that felt gooood...'

'Fuck your cum feels so warm.'

'That means you did a good job baby.'

I laid back down on the blanket and she went to the bathroom to clean herself. She came back laid down next to me and we both went to bed.

The next morning, I woke up with a throbbing headache, hard cock and no one by my side. I washed my face, brushed my teeth and showered. Opened my laptop and wrote four poems about how my current false sense of happiness was dependent on one-night stands and blurry weekends as I woke up every morning thinking about when all this pain will end meanwhile the woman, I thought was my one and only had now turned into one of many...I went downstairs to the hotel canteen ate a plate of pancakes and scrambled eggs, walked back up to my room and went to bed. I woke up to the feeling of someone pushing me. I opened my eyes and saw that it was Larry.

'It's almost 6.30 kid, wake up!'

'I don't know if I can read today...'

'It's only a hangover son, you'll get over it. I brought a glass of water and two paracetamols for you. Take them. How did it go last night?'

'Thank you. It went well I think...I like her. I liked her assertiveness.'

'Okay. That's good, I guess...Is she coming to the reading tonight?'

'I don't know. Haven't spoken to her yet.'

'Are you going to tell Jhené?'

'Man, can I even get in touch with Jhené?'

'Yeah, you right. Anyways you have thirty more minutes until Remy picks us up. Wake up and dress.'

'Okay.'

He left I took up phone and called Valeria.

'Hello?'

'Hey, it's Chuck from last night.'

'Hey Chuck, what are you up to?'

'Nothing much. Just getting ready for the reading tonight. Will you be there?'

'Okay. And no, I'm currently at work. I finish at 10 so if you want, we could meet up after?'

'Yes, that's fine. I'll text you the address to the hotel.'

'Okay cool. Bye.'

I took the two paracetamols and got ready.

I took a cab back to the hotel right after the reading. Valeria came thirty minutes later. We repeated last night except this time she came *twice*, and I came all over her breasts. I found myself liking her. Well at least more than I thought I would. And I found myself wanting to spend more time with her.

'You should come visit in me Paris. You could even spend a weekend or two...'

She sat on the edge of the bed turned around and looked at me.

'Chuck...this is *just* sex. Nothing more. I thought you knew.'

'Why can't it be anything more?'

'Because my heart wasn't made for love. It denies it whenever it comes.'

'But you said love is what you make it and with whom you make it with?'

'And you write poems about love. I guess in some way we're all *liars*...'

She went to the bathroom cleaned herself up came back and started dressing.

'No. Stay. At least give me that.'

'You're a great fuck so okay.'

'Is that all I am?'

'No. You're also a good person.'

'How do you know that?'

'Because a broken heart can always spot its *equal*.'

I wondered if there was a deeper meaning behind what she said, but a part of me didn't want to find out. She undressed got back in bed and we started kissing again. But this time it felt different. There was no enthusiasm or passion. Almost like two strangers being forced to kiss during a game of spin of the bottle with people spectating. A sense of guilt started eating up my consciousness. I started thinking about Sade as I turned around and tried to sleep. Was this how she felt? Worthless. Used. Wishing for a love that could never be reciprocated. Now I thought about Valeria as I could feel the warmth from her body next to me. What did she mean with a broken heart? Had she also once upon a time wished for a love that could never be reciprocated? Must be a frustrating feeling when men only like you for your body without realizing that under those mesmerizing eyes, lies a tragically beautiful story. Of a rose that grew up from concrete, the black sheep misunderstood in her family. The outcast, that could never fit into society. Surrounded by friends but always felt alone grew up with both parents and yet searched for a home. Gave up on love because for her all men were the same, got hurt once and promised herself never again. That's why she continues her lonesome journey, just her and her tragically beautiful story. To Sade, Célia, Valeria and Jhené I would like to apologize on behalf of all the ungrateful men in this world. You are too good for us, and this world would be a better place without us.

The next day I was yet again woken up by Larry's touch.

'Chuck...Chuck...Chuck!! Wake up kid, our flight leaves at 1.30'

'Ahhh fuckk...what's the time?'

'It's 10.20.'

'Why on earth did you wake me up so early then?'

'Better to be safe than sorry. Now get up. And have a shower. This whole room smells like pussy.'

We both started laughing loudly. He left and I checked my phone. I had four missed calls from Jhené. Fuck. I called her back. Ring...ring...ring...

'Hi Chuck.'

'Hey how are you feeling?'

'Much better thank you. How was the reading? I saw the clips that was posted on your fan page on Facebook. You did really good.'

'Thank you. I had a good feeling about it. Just didn't like the crowd.'

'You and your dislike for literature students.'

'They just piss me off Jhené. Bunch of people that think they're different or special when in reality they're just like everybody else in the room... Boring. Normal.'

'Okay Mr. anarchist don't go beating up innocent students now.'

'Someone woke up feeling like a comedian today.'

'Well...I've always been the funniest one out of us two. But on a serious note, we need to have a talk about us...a good talk though.'

The guilt started eating me up again and my mind started feeling heavy. I don't know where this guilt came from or when it started, but I didn't like it one bit. Why was I feeling bad when we both didn't even know if we were in a relationship or not? I considered not saying anything, but in the end, I decided that would be the kindest thing to do. I didn't consider myself a good or *honorable* man, but I tried my best to be as pure as possible. At least then there might be a slight possibility that God may let me into heaven or at least grant me safe passage to hell.

'Jhené. I have to tell you something...'

'What baby?'

'I met a girl here and we had sex...I'm sorry.'

'Don't apologize.'

'You're not angry?'

'No. Just disappointed…In a way I wish you were a bad guy…it hurts less to get your heart broken by a bad guy than a good one. At least with the bad one you can see it coming from a mile away…but with the good one it sneaks up on you during your sleep and stabs your heart with a knife…'

'I'm so sorry Jhené…I don't know why I'm like this…see it all started in my childhoo-'

'SHUT THE FUCK UP CHUCK!!! Just shut the fuck up…AND STOP ALWAYS MAKING FUCKING EXCUSES!! Yes, I understand you had a difficult upbringing but JESUS FUCKING CHRIST you can't continue to blame your bad choices and fuck ups in life on your childhood! Move on and grow the fuck up…'

'You're right…you're so fucking right…I'm sorry Jhené. Do you still want to talk to me? Please do. I like having you in my life. It was one of the few good things

I had going for me, and look how much I fucked it up...I don't *deserve* you...but I need you...'

'I don't know...we can talk about it when you come back. When are you coming back?'

'Our flight is leaving at 1.30 so I'll be in Paris between 4.30 and 5.'

'Fine.'

'Are you okay?'

'You ask if I'm okay when you know that I'm not...but at best I can say I'm not sad... just disappointed.'

She hung up the call.

9

I had a month off from reading. I tried writing, but it wasn't working. I would write between fifteen to twenty pages every night just to wake up the morning after and delete them all. I tried to fuck more and drink more in a desperate attempt to find some inspiration and yet nothing came out of it except for hogwash words that felt forced. Like a student writing an essay the day before its deadline. I tried comforting myself by thinking that a great writer knew when not to write but the truth was that I couldn't stop wanting to write. I needed to write... It was who I am and what made me. See Charles was a *nihilist* that despised everyone and longed for death but Chuck...Chuck was an anarchist that used words in his rebellious warfare against this *vain* and heartless system we call life. I was now going through a phase where my believes aligned more with Charles. Life had lost its meaning and I was now rejecting all the things that I once upon a time used to love dearly...women, alcohol and writing. The thought of meaningless sex disgusted me and the idea of having to form a relationship with another woman drained me. I no longer knew how I felt about love. I had experienced it a couple of times in my insignificant life. I have loved and been loved, and on both occasions, it was great and horrifying because of the fear and knowledge that it would *end* at some point. But in this generation human relationships don't work anyways. Only the first three months had any thrill in it. The butterflies, passion, physical attraction...you know the easy-going honeymoon phase. Then after a while the eagerness would slowly fade away, contentment would sink in and the participants would lose interest. Masks would be taken off and *real* people would reveal themselves...mood swings, mentally ill, pettiness, killers, rapists, the jealous, the malicious. Society had created its own monsters and they consumed each other. Hiding until both participants decided to let them loose and make it a duel to the *death*...the death of their love. I realized that the most one could wish for in a human relationship nowadays was two and a half years. Our heart is a clock that tells us when to love and when to stop and yet our mind tells us to keep going until we end up wasting each other's time. During my twenty-four years on this earth, I've learned that if you ever come across love, hold onto every moment and cherish the memories as if they were irreplaceable treasures, because that's what they are. Hold onto that love until it takes its last breath. I used to love *love* until I found out I'm bad at it. Now I spend my days reminiscing about it.

I had lost track of what day it was as I sat on my bed trying to finish a bottle of white Pinot Noir whiles watching a movie. I didn't watch movies often, but I had my favorites. The Godfather, Goodfellas, Casino, Scarface, King of New York. I especially had a strong liking for movies directed by Martin Scorsese, whom I personally regarded as the best director to ever work in the movie industry. I admired the way he would depict the religious views of guilt, redemption, faith and the concepts of machismo, nihilism, crime and the corruption and greed that defines the American government. I was re-watching Goodfellas when I heard a knock at the door. Adrìan walked in dressed in his grey checkered smart pants and a slim fit plain white tee.

'Hey man, what are you doing?'

I paused the movie and put the half empty bottle on the nightstand.

'Nothing much. Just watching Goodfellas. Why?'

'Just asking…I'm having dinner with Esther and her friend in the kitchen. Come join us. You've been glued to that bed the whole week.'

'I don't really feel like it.'

'I'm not leaving until you come. And you know me. I would never say something unless I mean it.'

'Fine. This is unfair by the way. Coming here and interrupting my peace…'

I pushed the duvet aside and stood up.

'Hey man, put on underwear! I swear you're always naked.'

'Well look around Adrìan, are we not in my room? With great emphasis on *my*.'

'Yeah whatever…just put on some clothes.'

I put on a pair of boxers, black trousers a white hoodie and walked into the kitchen with Adrian. Esther had her dark brown curls tied in a bun and was busy dishing out the spaghetti meatballs on four separate plates. I introduced myself to Eve and sat down at the table across from her. She had a pale round face, straight black hair, black leggings and a baggy brown tee.

'So, Charles, Esther told me that you used to study law. What happened?'

She had a raspy voice that instantly put me off. I've always been picky when it came to voices. I don't know why but it was something that could either make or break a conversation with me. A woman's greatest sin was having a voice that didn't fit her appearance.

'Nothing. I just found out that education was the greatest trick to fool mankind.'

'In what way?'

'In the sense that society makes us feel like we need it to the point where we risk our happiness and mental health in order to have it.'

'I disagree. I feel like our generation force this narrative of that we don't need a degree to be successful in life, when the reality is that we do. My parents worked too hard to move from India to France just for me to waste my life away pursuing something that may not be certain.'

'Nothing in life is certain nor promised. That degree you hold doesn't guarantee you a job in that exact field. I believe that every human is born with a talent, and as a *parent* it's your job to help your child discover and foster that talent. Not box them in and put them on a path they don't want to go down just because you feel it's the right thing to do. If my child decided to drop out and pursue a career as a rock artist, I would give him or her my full support.'

'Okay. Cool. What if your child becomes a failure?'

'No human is a failure in life. We all have a purpose, no matter how big or small our role is. And I would rather see my child *fail* doing something that makes them happy instead of succeeding at doing something that takes away their joy. This life is fragile and short, and the only thing guaranteed in this life is death and the rest is what you make it. It would be unfair of me to make my child live a life I want for them instead of creating a life they want for themselves...'

'See that's where you're wrong. The whole point about life is to work hard and create generational wealth so that your future children and grandchildren can live a good life where they are well off. And in order to do that you need a degree instead of chasing a useless dream of becoming a Rockstar. I'll be finished with my medical studies this June and I already have a job lined up at one of the major hospitals in Paris. I don't think I could ever be with someone that's a failure in life or is not earning the same or more than me.'

'It's a good thing you're not pretty...'

Adrìan and Esther stopped eating and turned their faces towards me, whiles Eve squinted her eyes and gave me a dirty look before she spoke again.

'What the fuck did you just say?'

'Nothing. Anyways, what is a good life to you?'

'A life where I don't need to worry or stress about money.'

'Okay...did you read my book?'

'Yes, I did. It's the number one book in the country and Esther told me to check it out so I did.'

'Did you like it?'

'Writing wise I did. You have a captivating style of writing. But I didn't understand the plot.'

'What do you mean?'

'I don't know...Like I don't understand why those three teenagers were rebelling in the first place. They all came from good homes parents with money and had access to everything good in life, and yet they weren't happy. Their anger seemed misplaced and *unjustified*.'

'Ahhh okay so you're one of those people...'

She put on a stern voice. 'What people?'

Esther turned her face to the side and looked at me.

'Chuck! Stop it!'

Eve started speaking again.

'No, it's fine Esther. Let him say it. What type of person am I Charles? Or should I say Chuck?'

'Call me Charles.'

'Okay then Charles. Since you seem to have me all figured out how about you tell me about myself? Isn't that what writers do? Make up stories and descriptions about people.'

'Well since you insist. Let me see...you came from a middle-class home up north, maybe Lille? No...okay hmm Amiens? Yes. Your family wasn't starving but your parents didn't have excess money for you to show off either. Which is why you were jealous of your friends and spent your adolescence hating your family for not financially enabling you to live the life your friends were living. You moved to Paris when you were eighteen worked a couple of jobs and lied about your upbringing to join a friend group consisting of rich girls that only cared about money and status. When you got in your in early twenties you saw your friends started getting into relationships and you found yourself a rich guy that didn't have time for you or anything in common with you, but you stayed with him because of who he was. Posting happy couple pictures on social media and yet going to bed most nights alone. You loved him more than he loved you, and you thought you carried more importance in his life when the truth is that he didn't give a fuck about you. Now you spend your days walking around and talking about how much you hate men and how peaceful life is without them, when the reality is that you're just a sad and *miserable* woman that can only find a false sense of happiness in money...'

Adrìan stared at me intensively whiles everybody else went silent.

'Chuck! Relax. That's enough. You've said what you needed to say.'

I continued staring at Eve. 'And see now you're giving me that look, like I just killed your cat. A look that tells me that I was spot on with everything I said...and now you're standing up and about to leave.'

She told Adrìan and Esther thank you for the food and started making her way towards the hallway before she turned around and spoke to me.

'YOU KNOW WHAT FUCK YOU CHARLES!! You're an asshole and a shitty writer! AND I TAKE BACK EVERYHING I SAID ABOUT YOUR BOOK...It was AWFUL and a piece of hot garbage!!'

I laughed as I shouted back. 'THANK YOU VERY MUCH. MAKE SURE TO BUY THE NEXT ONE TOO!'

She slammed the door and left. Esther stood up and started cleaning the table whiles Adrìan was still sitting down across from me. He smiled looked at me and shook his head.

'You're a fucked-up man Chuck…'

'Ohh come on, you can't tell me that wasn't funny. She practically asked for it.'

We both started laughing. 'Okay fine, I'm not going to lie it was funny. But damn was that necessary… What about her didn't you like?'

'Everything. But mostly her mind. I know I might come across as a *promiscuous* man…but shit even a prostitute got her standards and requirements.'

'Man, what's going on with you? You've just closed yourself in and barricaded yourself in your room almost the whole month. Are you going through something? Are you okay? The saddest part is that you haven't even written anything…you have all this talent and you're wasting away…'

'And you thought that would be fixed by trying to match me with someone?'

'Well, you can't blame a man for wanting to be a good friend.'

'I guess you're right...Where is Esther going?'

'I don't know. Probably calling Eve to clean up the chaos you just caused in this kitchen.'

'Hmm okay. Remind me to give her a hug next time I see her. If that's all I'll be going back to my room.'

I walked back in undressed and continued watching the movie.

I woke up the next morning and spent a couple of minutes staring at the blank page on my computer before I decided to close it. I walked into the kitchen opened the fridge and cracked open a beer. Walking back to my room I saw a letter on kitchen table with my name on it. I peeled it open and saw a wedding invitation. I stormed into my room picked up my phone and called Célia.

'Hi Chuck...how are yo-'

'Is this a sick joke or what is it?'

'What are you talking about?'

'The wedding invitation I just received. WHAT THE FUC-'

'Okay first of all don't you even dare have that tone with me, and I'm sorry I didn't mean for you to find out this way. I was going to call you.'

'Okay so why didn't I receive a call?'

'I don't know Chuck maybe because planning a wedding isn't easy? I've had a lot of shit to do you know.'

'FUCKING MATISSE, CÉLIA?? OUT OF ALL THE UNDERSERVING MEN IN THIS WORLD YOU CHOSE

THAT TEDIOUS AND UPTIGHT FUCK??? He's not even good for you.'

'DON'T YOU FUCKING COME HERE AND TALK ABOUT WHAT'S GOOD FOR ME!! You're the last person to speak on something like that. You blow your life away fucking everything that moves and try to drink yourself to death...'

'Okay, so what? At least I know that I'm good for you and that you love me...I know you Célia. He's a money loving suit wearing turd...he's everything you told me you didn't like...'

'He's *safe* Chuck...sometimes that's all a woman wants. Someone that's safe and stable.'

'And you're trying to say that I can't be that?'

'ARE YOU FUCKING JOKING?? Chuck, look at yourself. You're an emotional and impulsive wreck that can't face himself or reality. You always talk about how death is the only thing that will bring you happiness. Like what the fuck is that supposed to mean? Which woman would want to spend their life with a man that thinks like that?'

'Marry me.'

'Yes...WAIT WHAT??'

'I said marry me.'

'NO!! Chuck, listen to yourself...how can you love someone else when you can't even love yourself? And what happened? I thought you hated marriages. But listen to you know, being the biggest *cliché* of them all. I know you Chuc-'

'I don't know, and I don't care. Just don't marry that guy. He's a representation of everything that's wrong with this world...'

'Maybe yours, but he is perfect for my world.'

'Okay fine. Go on a date with me first and then decide after that.'

'CHUCK STOP IT!!! I'm going to hang up if you don't stop. I thought you were going to take this as an adult but clearly I was wrong.'

'I know you love me Célia and I know you will always do. Please don't do this. He will never love you or know you like I do. I know you Célia. Every side of you...I know what makes you cry, smile, angry, happy...I know your fears, traumas. I KNOW YOU...'

It went silent on the other end and I thought she had hung up.

'Hello??'

'I have to go Chuck...Let me know if you're coming or not...goodbye. Take care.'

She ended the call. I walked into the bathroom and saw my reflection in the mirror. I felt disgust, fear, sadness, pain, anger and a huge dose of regret. I felt like a broken child in an adult's body standing in the shower with the water pouring down on me struggling to comprehend the phone call that just took place. Men are merciless savages that prey on weak hearts and gullible minds to receive a love with the purpose of boosting their egos. Which is why their pride views it as a defeat whenever a former lover moves on to another man. Their reserved spot in the woman's heart is overtaken by another barbaric male until he himself is replaced. A vicious and cruel cycle indeed. But in a way it's a true representation of male love. Men desire women just for men to hurt women. A man could have three hundred and sixty-five girlfriends for each day of the year, and yet his pride would still take a beating when he finds out that he has been replaced. That's why we're reluctant to put all our eggs in one basket, instead slicing a piece of our heart handing it to each lover we come across in this life leaving a trail of blood behind. Some might earn a bigger piece than others, but no one will ever have the whole thing. Safety in numbers is what we're taught from an early age. I started reminiscing about the women I wanted to love and those that I loved. I wondered how big of slice each of them had cut out, and if I even had any slices left. Stepping out of the shower a part of me felt the need to find out. I wanted to call Jhené...

10

Serhan was busy serving customers as I walked into the restaurant and sat at the table close to the window that looked out towards the street. He saw me walk in nodded his head and smiled. It had been a while since I last visited Cappadocia, and it felt good to be back again in a somewhat familiar environment. I opened the menu pretending to be intensively reading and thinking about what I was going to order, when Aydin strolled towards me with a cup of chai tea. He had a certain glow on his face as he took a seat across from me.

'Our famous writer has returned home!'

'Don't flatter me Aydin...I might just be the most *unfamous* famous writer then if that's the case.'

'Well anyhow. Everybody here is *proud* of you Chuck. Serhan, Fatma and I have all read your book. Fatma loved it.'

'Thank you. Proud is not a word I'm used to hearing... How is everybody?'

'We're all okay. Diren is enjoying her first year at university which is grea-'

'What does she study again?'

'Computer science at the university in Rennes. Don't get me wrong it's a good school, but no father wants their daughter to move too far away from home.'

'A lot of evil men in this world.'

'A lot of evil of *everybody* in this world...no soul is pure anymore, Chuck. In one way or another we're all tainted with something bad.'

'So how then can you know if someone is good or evil?'

'If they're seeking the light or chose to embrace darkness. Well at least according to the teachings of Islam.'

'Do you honestly think that all the answers we seek on this earth can be found in a book written over a thousand years ago?'

'It depends on the questions you want to ask, my son. In a world filled with hopelessness and despair we all need something or someone to lean on, and who can support you better than the God himself that created you?'

'Fair enough. But why do pastors always talk about how sinners are destined for hell because they don't have a relationship with God, or how a lot of Christians are false for not having a good enough relationship with their God and not doing enough to maintain that relationship?'

'Sadly, I'm a Muslim and not Christian so I can't answer that question. But I'll tell you this much, your relationship with God is between you and him alone. No man, pastor, imam or rabbi can tell you how that relationship should be or define that relationship for you. We all believe in the same God, just in different ways. As it should be. God can take many shapes and forms according to what our *needs* are. Some of us need a God that's strict because we're lazy, merciful because we've lived an evil past, compassionate because we're trying, and one that's just *present*

because we desperately need something to believe in.'

'Do you think it's ever too late to ask for forgiveness?'

'Do you know what's so great about Islam?'

'No.'

'We have something called tawba which in essence is the Islamic concept of repentance. In Islam no one is perfect except for Allah, and he does not require us to be that either. Any human can make mistakes, with Allah being the only one that can forgive you. When you ask for forgiveness by performing an act of tawba Allah will generally accept it as long as it is sincere and genuine...It's okay to commit mistakes Chuck, as long as you make a conscious choice of not doing it again.'

'Okay.'

'Have you made any?'

'I don't know...I feel like that's all I've been doing lately. I try not to live a life with regrets but it's getting harder and harder for each day that passes by.'

'Ask for forgiveness and repent, my son...it's never too late.'

Fatma walked over gave me a hug from behind and a kiss on the cheek.

'Hi, my baby, how are you?'

'I'm okay Fatma. What about you?'

'Just tired. Been a long and busy day today. Sorry to interrupt your conversation Chuck, I just came over to talk to Aydin.'

'That's alright.'

She spoke to Aydin in Turkish but from the looks of it, it seemed like it had something to do with whatever was going on in the back of the kitchen. She walked away and Aydin stood up from the chair.

'Sorry Chuck I have to get back to the kitchen. Usman is my nephew and I love him, but that boy couldn't make food to save his life. Just stop by whenever you want to and always remember that this place is your home too. We all love you here.'

He left and I finished my chai tea. Sitting there alone I wanted to correct my wrongs, but I didn't know where to start. I wanted to call Sade, but I had no way of contacting her ever since she blocked me. In the end I decided to start with Jhené.

The cab arrived and I gave the driver the address to her apartment. I was deciding whether to call or text her in order for her to let me in through the intercom until I saw a man walk out the main building door and I ran before the door could shut itself. I took the elevator up and knocked on apartment 377. I knocked four-five times without anyone opening up, and it seemed as if no one was home until I heard the sound of locks turning. She had on black knee cut denim jeans, dark grey sweater and her dreadlocks tied in an updo bun with strands of hair hanging down.

'Hi Jhen-'

'What do you want?'

'To talk and to apologize.'

'It's okay.'

She halfway closed the door forcing me to push it back open.

'Jhené please hear me out!'

We walked in and she went over to the kitchen counter and opened the cabinet.

'Do you want anything to drink?'

'No thank you. I just wanted to come over here and apologize for the way I treated you and how I left things between us.'

She didn't reply. Instead, she reached into the cabinet took out a plate and launched it at me. I quickly ducked behind the kitchen table.

'YOU SON OF A BITCH!! AFTER ALL THESE MONTHS THAT'S THE BEST YOU COULD COME UP WITH???'

After throwing two-three plates she opened the drawer and started running through the utensils. She had a strong preference for knives.

'YOU USELESS PIECE OF SCUM!! I FUCKING HATE YOU!! HOW FUCKING DARE YOU COME TO MY PLACE AFTER CHEATING ON ME!!'

The attack stopped and I peeked up and saw that she was now standing next to the sink sobbing with her hands covering her face. I walked over and forced my arms around her whiles she kept trying to pull herself away.

'I'm sorry Jhené. For everything...'

She started pounding my chest as she continued to cry. I drew her closer to me.

'Jhené stop...STOP! I'm sorry for what I did and for the hurt it must've caused you. You were going through a difficult time and I wasn't there for you. I wasn't the boyfriend or friend I needed to be...your love was *complicated*, but it was nonetheless good. And I took it for granted.'

The pounding stopped. I could feel her tears on my white tee.

'I don't know in some ways I wish I could go back in time and undo the mistake I did but in other ways I don't. Because hurting you made me realize how much I needed you.'

She looked up in an attempt to catch eye contact with me. 'Do you still need me?'

'I do but in a different way.'

'In what way?'

'I don't know…in a friendly way?'

She took a step back and released herself from my grip.

'WOOOW you got some balls Chuck. You're indeed a confusing man. You come all this way and do all this just to ask me to be your friend? What kind of twisted world do you live in?'

'Listen, I don't mean it a noncaring way. It's just that I've never had a genuine friend that was a woman, and I don't want to lose you either. I don't know if I can ever be the *right* man for you. But I hope I can do a better job as a friend. I don't want to hurt you again Jhené. In fact, I don't want to hurt anyone again. You deserve a man that's going to appreciate your love the way it deserves to. I don't know if I can handle that responsibility again...'

'I appreciate the maturity and honesty, I guess. What is this, a Chuck 2.0 or what?'

'Just a Chuck that decided to give life a second chance by doing it right this time. Instead of sitting around and waiting for death I might as well embrace being alive.'

'That's good. I'm happy for you Chuck. I really am. You have so much good in you that deserves to be showcased instead of the bad.'

'Thank you. How is everything, had any episodes lately?'

'Just a couple here and there. They gave me a new medication that seems to be working. What about you, you working on a new book?'

'That's good. No. I haven't really written anything in the past few months.'

'Why not?'

'I guess writers block finally caught up to me.'

She gave me a peck on the cheek. 'You might not be a good lover but there's no doubt that you're a great writer. Don't worry. Everything will be okay again.'

'I certainly hope so.'

'Anyways I have to go redo my makeup and get ready for work. I'm already behind schedule. But when can I see you again?'

'I have a reading in London, but I can let you know when I get back?'

She leaned in again and we shared a long and passionate kiss.

'Do that.'

I found a bar that was a couple of blocks down the road from her apartment. It was midday on a Tuesday which was visible by the place being somewhat empty and quiet except for the indie rock music that was playing in the background. I ordered a glass of gin and tonic and found myself an empty booth. I picked up my phone fiddling around on it looking at old text messages and pictures before I finally gathered up the courage needed to call Célia.

Ring...ring...ring...ring...I almost thought it would go to voicemail until I heard someone speak.

'Hello.'

'Hi Célia. It's Chuck.'

'I know. I can tell. What's up?'

'Nothing much. Just wanted to let you know that I can't come to your wedding bu-'

'Okay. Bye.'

'Wait. Hold on! But from the bottom of my heart, I wish you and Matisse all the best. I hope he can be the man I couldn't be, and give you the future I failed to provide...It's sa-'

'Where's all this coming from?'

'From a place of *repentance* and regret, I guess. I've never stopped loving you Célia...and I don't think I ever will. But I know that I want the absolute best for you, and sadly enough I don't think I can be that for you. Well, I know I can't be that for you since you're marrying another man. But I hope at least we can be friends.'

'I don't know what to say Chuck. I didn't expect this. I'm in kind of a shock to be honest...'

'It's okay. You don't need to say anything. I just wanted to apologize for the man I was and the man I couldn't be.'

'I'm sad now...'

'Why?'

'I don't know. There's something about your voice when you're apologetic. It's hard to stay angry at you Charles Johnson...'

'Yeah, who knows maybe I should've done it more when we were together. Maybe it would've been different then.'

'Do you think so?'

'I do. Don't you?'

'I don't know, I guess. Like there are days where I miss you...I miss us. Some might look at what we had and call it toxic, but they would never understand what we had. Yes, there were bad times. but I would be lying if I said you didn't make me feel *special*. We had some great times together when you were not stubborn and childish.'

'It's funny how the mind easily remembers the bad but struggles to bring back the good.'

'It really is. You're a one-of-a-kind man, Chuck. I don't think I'll ever meet another man like you. And I don't know if that's good or bad...'

'What, are you second guessing your decision?'

'Honestly I don't know. I think our last conversation and this call right here just threw me off a bit. I don't know if I'm unsure, insecure or afraid. I haven't seen you since Henry's funeral. So, I don't know how I would react if I saw you again…But if you want, we can still meet up?'

'I don't think that would be a great idea.'

'Wow. Chuck apologizing and saying no to meeting a woman on the same day. The world must be coming to an end.'

We both laughed before I spoke again. 'No. I just don't want to fuck it up again.'

'Fuck what up again?'

'Your chance at true love and happiness…'

'That's very sweet of you…ARRGHH I FUCKING HATE YOU CHUCK!! Every time I think that I've finally managed to release myself from the bondage you have over me, you manage to suck me back in…'

'Okay then, how about this. Let's make a pact from now and until we die.'

'Here you go again being crazy. What pact?'

'If you're ever unhappy with Matisse, just give me a call and I will come swoop you up.'

'On what? Your skateboard?'

'Ahhh that's really funny. I almost forgot about your dry sense of humor. I'm actually in the process of getting my license you know.'

'That's good. Call me when you do.'

'Okay baby. I'll leave you now. Congratulations on your wedding. Love you.'

'Thank you, Chuck. Love you too.'

I laid my phone down on the table and continued drinking the gin and tonic. Wish you were here by Neck Deep was playing in the background. The lyrics of the song threw me into a state of reminiscence. The saying of you don't know what you have until it's gone, is a big fucking cliché. But it's nonetheless the truth. I had two chances at love, and I blew it. I didn't know where to go from here, but at least I knew that a small part of my soul had been restored. I couldn't care less about an argument with a man. I've been in too many fights to not care. But a woman hating or being angry at me was different. That shit would eat me up daily. Piercing my heart when I was awake and hunting my dreams when I was at sleep. A woman's wraith is an anger that is felt more than it is seen. Men are different. A man that's angry will not hide that anger from the world, showing it through our facial expressions, body language, words and actions. But women. They will let their anger linger in the air, *following* you around everywhere you go. You can be in their presence and yet feel like a total stranger. Like there's an invisible wall blocking you from seeing the real her. Similar to chameleons they can adapt to any situation they're in as a defense mechanism to hide their true emotions. It's frustrating and yet admirable at the same time. A man has to know himself and know what he did wrong in order for the spell to disappear and the woman can reveal her true self.

She walked over to my booth sat across from me and placed my book on the table.

'I must say you look better in person.'

She was dressed in all funeral black with a silk dress a long leather trench coat and knee-high work boots. Her pale skin and fiery red dyed hair gave her a sex appeal that would show itself in her voice, walk and body movement.

'I don't know if that's a compliment or not.'

'Well, I walked all the way over here. So, take a guess.'

'Okay. Cool.'

'You don't seem that excited to have a beautiful woman in your presence.'

'Look around. We're in Paris. There's a beautiful woman in every corner of the city. After a while the beauty fades away and a man can no longer separate them from each other except by the way they make him feel. Almost like a new dish you're excited about cooking, and after all the labor and effort you sit down to eat the food and all of a sudden, your appetite is *gone*. That's what beauty is. It looks tempting when you don't have it until you get it, and you notice that you're no longer craving it.'

'You really do have a way with words huh.'

'I wouldn't be an author if I didn't.'

'I think I'm going to leave...'

She picked up the book and stood up. I reached out and took a hold of her hand.

'I'm sorry for the rudeness. Sit back down and keep me company. It's not a good thing to leave a man alone when he's feeling the blues.'

She flicked her hair and sat back down.

'Okay.'

'Do you want anything to drink?'

'Sure. I'll have a sex on the beach.'

I walked over to the bar ordered her cocktail and returned back to the booth.

'Now that we got the drink out of the way. What's your name?'

'Thank you. And my name is Geneviève, but most people just call me Gen or Viv.'

'I can't explain why but your name suits your appearance. You don't find that often. Let's toast to your parents for an achievement like no other.'

She let out a whispering giggle that showcased her bright smile and high raised cheekbones as she lifted her glass to touch mine.

'It's a pleasure to meet you Viv. My name is Chuck.'

'But your book says Charles?'

'I know. I never really liked that name. Which is why I prefer Chuck.'

'Why don't you like it?'

'Because my father gave me that name.'

'Ahhh okay a writer with parental issues. Truly living up to the stereotype huh.'

'Well in a way don't we all have issues.'

'I guess so.'

'So, what do you do?'

'I'm a student.'

'What do you study?'

'Electronic engineering.'

'Do you like it?'

'Fuck no I hate it!'

'So why do you do it?'

'Sadly, enough I do it to please my parents. I come from a very conservative and religious home where education is the only thing they care about aside from God.'

'So, you're telling me that you spend the only chance at life you'll ever have doing something you don't want to just to please people that will most likely die before you? I hate life, but you're a *slave* to it.'

'Nooo Chuck, like you actually don't understand. I can't even wear jewelry or dress in certain clothes whenever I go back home. Like I have to take off my earrings and hide my tattoos every time I meet up with them.'

'Do you do it out of fear or are you afraid that they will be disappointed in you?'

'I think it's more so out of *judgement*. I've come to accept their disappointment. That's nothing new. I'm just tired of the judgement. You know when I was young, I used to think my parents hated me.'

'Why?'

'Because it seemed like they favored my other siblings. They would brag about how intelligent my sister was or about my musically gifted brother. But with me it was different... The worst part is that my siblings are only two-three years younger than me, and yet my parents would blame me whenever my siblings fucked up or something happened to them. I don't know. I always felt like an outcast. I don't think they hate me, but I feel like they aren't able to accept me because I'm so unlike them. I don't share the same values or views with anyone in my family... What about you? Did you ever feel like you were forced to be in a place where you don't belong?'

'Yes. I feel that every day.'

'Where is yours?'

'This earth.'

'Life must be painful for you then.'

'Alcohol helps. And fucking too.'

'You love sex?'

'More than the average whore I think.'

'Which part of sex do you like?'

'It depends on the woman. But a good foreplay and a great head is always appreciated.'

'Do every woman give great head?'

'Some can. *Most* don't.'

'Okay. What do you think about me?'

'I think you're a sex freak.'

'What gives you that impression?'

'Because you're just like me. You fuck to *rebel*. You're rebelling against the shackles your parents have around your neck...whiles I'm rebelling against something totally different.'

'Like what?'

'Life.'

'Do you live far from here?'

'We would have to take two buses or a cab.'

'We can drive. My car is parked right outside.'

'But you've been drinking?'

'And here I was thinking you was this bad boy rebel. I don't know if I want to fuck you anymore.'

'Okay. Fine. Let's go.'

She threw her jacket on the bed and was standing on my skateboard trying to make it turn sideways.

'Aren't you a little bit too old to be skating?'

I raised up from my slouched position on the bed and looked at her. 'I didn't know there was an age limit on fun.'

'Ohh okay sorry Mr. sensitive. I was just asking. I wonder how many girls have been in this room.'

'Why do you care?'

'Because I want to know what type of girls the man I'm going to *fuck* likes.'

'And who says I want to fuck you?'

'Ohhh please your eyes have practically been undressing me the whole evening...'

'And yours haven't?'

'They have. I'm not afraid to admit that. But I want to see it first.'

'See what?'

'Your cock. Stand up and pull it out.'

'Are you crazy?'

'No. I'm fun. Now do it.'

Her brazenness turned me on. I stood up from the bed unbuckled my belt pulled my jeans down and dragged my cock out.

'Not necessarily my proudest moment...'

'Yeah, I can see that. Why is it so soft and just hanging there?'

'Because I'm not hard. Anyways it's my turn to tell you what to do.'

'Okay. Go on.'

'Lay on the bed and touch yourself.'

'Fine let me take off my dress.'

'No. Leave it on.'

She laid down on the bed slipped her dress halfway up to her thigh shoved her hand down her red thong and started touching herself as she closed her eyes.

'Keep your eyes open and look at me.'

We maintained eye contact her touching herself and me stroking my cock. I started getting hard. She kept making sounds. Her moaning got louder, and my cock got harder. She played with her breasts softly rubbing her perky nipples. I walked over grabbed her head and shoved her mouth down my cock. I held her head as she went to work choking on it and only releasing her grip to breathe out as the built-up saliva dripped down my cock and hit the carpet on the ground. She softly licked my balls with her tongue whiles stroking my cock with her hand. She continued the motion until I couldn't take it no more. I got on top of her pushed her legs apart slid her panties to the side and mounted my cock in.

'ARRGHHH FUCK YOU'RE BIGGG!'

I started thrusting like it was the last fuck I would ever have, as if death awaited me at *climax*. I switched between fast and slow as I glided my cock up and down in an attempt to hit her g-spot. I don't know why but my cock being in her warm cunt turned me into a madman that didn't have no filter or care in the world.

'AWWW YEAH YOU LIKE THAT YOU FUCKING WHORE!!'

She pulled me closer and I could feel her nails dig into my back. 'AWW YESSS CHUCK FUCK MeeeEEE THAT FEELS SO GOOD!!!'

'Who's fucking pussy is this!?!?'

'It's yours Chuck AHHH FUCK ME IT'S YOURS BABYYY IT'S FUCKING YOURSSSsss.'

She lifted both of her legs and laid them on my shoulder as I started choking her with my hands.

'LOOK AT ME YOU FUCKING SLUT...YOU LIKE THAT HUHH?!?!'

'YESS CHUCK I DO OH MY FUCKING GOD I DOOO please don't stop AHHH DON'T STOOOOPP.'

My phone started ringing I released my grip from around her neck and reach down towards my jeans to get it wondering who in their right mind would call me at this time. It was Larry.

'Hello?'

'Hey kid just wanted to call and make sure you have everything ready for our flight tomorrow.'

'I do.'

'You sure? You packed? You have your passport rea-'

'Larry! I do. Everything is ready.'

'Okay man, just asking. Man, I can't wait. You should be proud of yourself. Reading at Oxford University is something spe-'

'Larry please. Now is really not the time.'

'Why not?'

'Because I'm busy.'

'Doing what?'

'Take one guess Larry.'

'Well, I know it's not writing so then it must be...OHHHH okay. My apologies. Have fun kid. Just make sure you're well rested for tomorrow.'

'See you man.'

I hung up and went back to work. She sat on top of me threw her head back and arched her back as she started riding me back and forth. She started making noises again. The moaning became louder and my cock got harder. I didn't know how long I could go on for. I needed to cum but at the same time I didn't want to. I was facing an internal dilemma as I watched her breasts bounce up and down together with her body. I tried my best to hold on for as long as I could but in the end, I lost control. I could feel the blood rushing and my cock almost exploding. I drew her close to me held her body tight and pounded her until I neared climax.

'GET UP I'M ABOUT TO CUMMMM AHHHHH FUUUUckkkkKK!!'

She quickly rose up and I came all over my stomach almost reaching my chest. She smiled bent down stuck her tongue out and licked the cum off my cock and body before standing up and walking to the bathroom. She came back in and started dressing.

'What are you doing?'

'What does it look like? I'm leaving.'

'Why?'

'Come on Chuck...I figured this was a one-time thing. You don't really strike me as the repetitive type.'

'Well, that's an unfair judgement on your part. How about next time I take you on a proper date. Old fashion style wine and dine.'

'Okay. When?'

'I'm travelling tomorrow but I'll be back on Friday. So, how about Saturday?'

'Okay that works. When is your flight?'

'Like 12.45.'

'Okay. I got to get going I have a 9am class tomorrow. But call me when you get back.'

'Sure.'

She finished dressing walked over to the bed kissed me and left.

I took a sip from my glass with rum and coke as I looked out towards the cloud of skies that covered the ground beneath the plane. I leaned my head against the window and thought about how it would feel to live life as a bird. Having the ability to spread your wings and fly away whenever life became hard. Living every day in "do not disturb mode" …soaring so high up in the sky that no one can contact or reach you. Flying from place to place without any sense of direction in a reckless attempt to flee from the hardships of life, the pain you encounter in life and ultimately the people that make up your life. I think we all have days where we look up and envy those creatures gliding through the skies that tower over us flapping their feathers towards their hopeless destination running from whichever mess they left behind. I took another sip and pondered upon what bird I would be...maybe a crow? Or a sparrow? No...hmm how about a dove? No...no...no... AHAA, I got it. A bald eagle. The king of the sky. Soaring the skies alone as it spends its life safeguarding its throne. A deadly and yet lazy animal. A true opportunist, feeding off already dead animals in order to not expend much of their energy.

'What are you thinking of?'

Larry tapped my shoulder multiple times trying to get my attention. 'Chuck...Chuck...what are you thinking of kid?'

'Ohhh nothing much. Just birds. Do you sometimes wish you could fly away from this earth?'

'I don't think we would be humans if we didn't.'

I whispered in a low voice. 'Lucky ass birds...'

'I thought you were thinking about the woman from yesterday. Who was she?'

'Some chick I met at a bar...'

'Do you like her?'

'I don't know yet. We're going on a date on Saturday.'

'Ohhhh Chuck taking a girl out on a date...'

'Why does that seem to shock everyone lately?'

'I don't know, maybe it's because most of your girls don't last long enough for me to hear about them twice.'

'Fair enough. Wish me better luck this time then.'

'Francesca and I have been talking, we're considering going back to the States.'

'How long?'

'For good... You should come with us Chuck. I can get you reading gigs there too.'

'I don't know man. I don't know if I'm ready to move...'

'Life never waits for us to be ready, son. Look at yourself. Paris is not good for your mental health. Sometimes you need to step out of your comfort zone in order for a better version of you to come alive.'

'You're a true optimist for believing that people can create better versions of themselves.'

'Well, isn't that what life is about? A lonesome journey in which you discover different sides of yourself...both the good and the bad.'

'Ohh wow that was really deep, Larry. Where is all this *sapience* coming from?'

'Experience, kid. You might regard yourself as an old soul, but I've lived an old lif-'

Larry was interrupted by a voice ringing out of the speakers. It was an announcement from one of the flight attendants.

LADIES AND GENTLEMEN, AS WE START OUR DESCENT TOWARDS HEATHROW AIRPORT PLEASE MAKE SURE YOUR SEAT BACKS AND TRAY TABLES ARE IN THEIR FULL UPRIGHT POSITION. MAKE SURE YOUR SEAT BELT IS SECURILY FASTENED AND ALL CARRY-ON LUGGAGE IS STOWED UNDERNEATH THE SEAT IN FRONT OF YOU OR IN THE OVERHEAD BINS. THANK YOU.

11

Once upon a time I wrote a book called Rebels without
a cause. People seemed to dig it, so I wrote two more
and ended up whoring myself out to an industry in
which the public was my pimp and their opinion
determined how much I would charge my customers.
Selling my body page by page reading after reading,
whiles slowly but surely starting to feel like an over-
fucked flappy cunt. Nonetheless I couldn't complain.
Being a literature harlot did have its perks. It paid the
bills, provided excess money to buy alcohol and a
surplus of female readers that would fuck me based off
my writing alone. I don't know if I was using the
industry or if it was using me. But I guess it was a fair
trade since we both got what we wanted. It sucked me
dry, and I sucked as many tits as I could.

I woke up and sat on the edge of the bed. I picked up my phone and looked at the date. It was May 26th. My birthday. I had a strong dislike for birthdays...especially mine...deeply rooted in the fact that I never celebrated it with my parents nor my family. Instead, my grandmother would give me 20 euros which I would take to the nearest Turkish shop and order a döner kebab together with Henry and the rest of the boys. Most people celebrated birthdays as another year of evading death and exploring their continuous lust for life...whiles the cheerless spirits like me dreaded the day it arrived as we got to witness another year of death and freedom pass us by. Twenty-six years old. Looking back at my life I never thought I would reach past the age of twenty-five. I was hoping death would've been kind to me by then and ended my suffering. But who was I kidding the grim reaper was a sadistic and perverted character that came for the hearts that didn't deserve it and neglected the souls that yearned for it. I was scrolling through my birthday messages when I got a call from Larry.

'Hello?'

'Happy birthday to you... Happy birthday to you.... Happy birthday dear Ch-'

'Thank you, Larry. You can spare me the singing.'

'Since it's your birthday I'm going to allow the rudeness. So, how's the birthday boy feeling?'

'Okay, I guess. Could be better could be worse.'

'Well then I got something that'll cheer you up.'

'What?'

'Hollywood is calling for you Chuck.'

'What's that supposed to mean?'

'I got a call two days ago from a director that wants to turn your book into a miniseries.'

'Which book?'

'The second one. Blame it on our youth.'

'Wait what?! Out of all the books, that's the one that peaked their interest? Honestly thought it would've been the third or the first one.'

'Hey! They want it and we got it. That's the only thing that matters. So, what do you think? Should we move forward with it?'

'If you think we should then I don't see any reason why not to. What's the name of the director?'

'Okay. Hold on give me a sec I need to check my email…. AHA here it is. His name i-'

'Larry sorry to interrupt but can I call you back? Viv is calling.'

'Yeah, no problem kid. Go enjoy your birthday, we'll talk business another day. Proud of you, son.'

I ended the call with Larry and accepted Viv's.

'Hello.'

'HAPPY BIRTHDAYYY BABYYYY!'

'Thank you. I appreciate the text you sent too. It put a smile on a sad soul.'

'No worries. How are you feeling?'

'You know...the usual.'

'Let me guess. Could be better could be worse?'

'You're starting to know me all too well baby.'

'Well then hopefully you'll like what I'm making for you.'

'What is it?'

'I can't tell you! It's a surprise. And when you taste it be honest and don't lie to me.'

'Okay. I won't.'

'Good. When are you coming?'

'Around 8, I think. Do you want me to bring anything?'

'Chuck it's your birthday. Don't worry. I got everything sorted.'

'Alright. See you later. Love you.'

'Love you too.'

A year and some months had gone by and she was still very much in my life. In an unexplainable way I had managed to become addicted to her presence and how it made me feel and the emotional safety it provided me with. She was the refuge I sought whenever the worries in life came chasing after me with a knife. I was infatuated with her beauty but fell in love with her mind. See I wrote poems about how much I hated this world, whiles she spoke about it. We were different in some ways but similar in most. She understood and accepted me for what I was and what I couldn't be.

Two lunatics racing towards death in an attempt to run away from a moralist society. We never spoke about what we were or tried to define the unconventional relationship we had. She didn't ask me about the lovers in my life and I didn't pry into hers and yet we both knew where we had each other. She brought out a side of me I had stowed away ever since Célia and I broke up. I could feel it whenever I was around her. The irresistible need to touch and feel her warmth with the way she fucked being art and my cock and her cunt the paintbrushes she used to create a masterpiece on the bed that was her canvas. The jealousy in me that would expose itself when a man spoke to her in public or would blow up her phone whenever we were together. Nonetheless there were different types of jealousy. And this one wasn't as embarrassing and emotionally vulnerable compared to its counterpart. Bad jealousy was the fear and thought of her fucking the men that showed her attention on the street or called her phone

287

when I wasn't around. Whiles good jealousy was the horror of her removing my disguise and seeing me for the ugly and degenerate fuck I pretended not to be as she slowly realized that she could do much better. And my jealousy was a mixture of both...but mostly the latter.

I was in the elevator on my way up to her apartment as I stood there watching my reflection in the mirror. I was a year older and yet not much had changed except for the length of my dreadlocks that was now tied in a bun with strands of hair hanging down covering parts of my face. I wore my black converses, black pants a white vest that was tucked in and a floral button-down shirt that was casually open. The elevator opened up I took a left and walked down the hallway until I reached apartment 29. She walked in first and I was right behind admiring the way her red dress tightly wrapped itself around and brought forth her pear-shaped body. She had a medium sized studio apartment with clean white walls a queen-sized bed a desk with her computer and candles on it and a sliding closet opposite the bed. She had a small cut out bookshelf above her bed with fairy lights going around it. I noticed all three of my books on the bookshelf as I turned around looked at her and smiled whiles she was busy prepping the food. An avid reader of my work she had turned into my literary muse being the first to read the poems and books I wrote before they went public. I walked over and hugged her from the back.

'What did you cook?'

'Pad kee mao. I saw it in a series I was watching and thought you might like it.'

'Does it have prawns in it?'

'Yes, it does. Don't worry I know how much you love your prawns.'

'I wrote a poem for you on the way here.'

She turned around and faced me. 'Really? Okay let's eat and then you read it for me.'

'I thought I would just message it to you.'

'Nooooo. I want you to read it for me. Like properly read it. The way you read at your shows.'

'Okay baby.'

'Where do you want to eat? The bed or the floor?'

'Anywhere is fine with me.'

'Okay. I'll lay the blanket down and we'll sit on the floor and eat. I'll turn off the main light and leave the fairy lights on.'

She put the noodles in two separate bowls and poured us two glasses of white wine. I laid the black fleece blanket on the ground and we started eating as we sat opposite each other.

'Mhmm this tastes really good.'

'Thank you. And see I can cook. It's just that school takes up most of my time, so I just prefer frozen food.'

'Your course makes me feel lazy for thinking law school was hard.'

'Dropping out worked out for you in the end, so you made the right choice. Have you made any birthday wishes?'

'I don't have any.'

'Okay. Let me try again. Is there anything you're thankful for this year leading up to your birthday?'

I hesitated to give a reply as I thought about it. Although I loathed my existence I would be lying if I didn't have anything to be thankful for. I wasn't necessarily proud of the choices I've made in life, but at least it gave me something to write about and a modest career I could live off. I've come to realize that living isn't so bad when you try and give it a shot...but as with anything else in life the hardest part is *trying*. Because trying implies that happiness might not come soon or even come at all.

'I think I'm thankful for life.'

'Which part of it?'

'All of it, I guess. Everything is strange. Life. People. And yet it's the strangeness and uncertainty of it that makes life what it is.'

'And what is life?'

'I don't quite know what life is, but I know it's not a course with textbooks and answers. Rather so I think it's an experience that is usually more felt than seen. An experience you can't plan or foresee. But then again what do I know. I'll just have to ask the Gods when I arrive at the gates of hell or heaven...whichever one opens first.'

'A man that's thankful for life and yet spends it thinking about death. You're indeed a complex man, Chuck.'

'Humans are fucked up beings. I'm just a bad at hiding it.'

'I think I've figured it out...'

'Figured out what?'

'What your main problem is.'

'And what is that?'

'You love women, but you hate yourself. So, the woman that ends up falling in love with you is a fool that's destined to get her heart broken. You hate yourself so much that your mind has convinced you that you don't deserve anything good. That's why you self-sabotage whenever a good woman comes into your life. You're not mean to women and you don't intentionally hurt them, but your mind creates absurd standards that no women could ever live up to just because it doesn't want you to fall in love.'

'So, would you consider yourself a fool?'

'Would it really be love if it didn't have the potential to drive us mad?'

'You should become a writer.'

'I'm already fucking one. I've paid my dues to the literary society. Okay I'm done eating. Can you read me the poem now?'

'Do I have to?'

'Yes, my handsome old man.'

'You're only four years younger than me. And okay, where do you want to sit?'

'I'll sit on the bed and you stand in front of me. Hold on let me go get your mic.'

She picked up the empty bowls put them in the sink handed me a wooden spoon and sat on the bed with her legs crossed. I stood in front of her with the wooden spoon close to my mouth and read

An old soul

And yet you bring out my inner child

Staring into your eyes as your lips touch mine

Is the secret to make a sane heart turn wild

Laying under the blanket

Talking about our dreams hopes and goals

Creating our own world

And a safe space for our lost souls

A world where it's only me and you

Running around

Being crazy

And everything else we want to do

Two rebels without a cause

Attempting to reignite their lust for life

Accepting each other's flaws

And revealing secrets we would usually hide

A sad writer's muse

With a presence he seeks whenever he's feeling the blues

You're more than what the mirror reflects

Beautiful

Intelligent

Soulful

Rebellious

Geneviève

You're that and everything else

Tears were streaming from her eyes as she spoke. 'Oh my God Chuck...I don't know what to say. Thank you...honestly that was really beautiful. Like I love it...I'm even crying. What's the title of the poem?'

'That's good. I'm glad you liked it. It's called a lost soul's muse.'

She walked over embraced me with her arms as she looked up into my eyes.

'I love that title. And I love you.'

We shared a long kiss before I lifted her by her thighs and moved over to the bed. That night she created a masterpiece even van Gogh would be envious of.

I was in the cab on my way home from the airport after a reading in Lyon when I could feel my phone vibrating. I looked at it as it continued ringing undecided if I should answer a number I didn't recognize. In the end I accepted the call.

'Hello?'

'Hi is this Chuck?'

'Yes, it is. Who am I speaking to?'

'Ohh hey Chuck it's Valeria.'

'Ahh okay. Hi Valeria. How are you?'

'I'm doing fine, thank you. I was just wondering if you were still in Paris?'

'Sadly yes. How come?'

'Okay. I'm coming to Paris this weekend, and was just wondering if you wanted to meet up?'

'Sure. Are you coming alone or?'

'Yes I am. I'm in dire need of a break from work and Strasbourg.'

'That's understandable. Are you staying at a hotel? If not, you could spend the weekend at my apartment. I only have one bed so we would have to sleep together. If that's okay?'

'You've already seen me naked, so it isn't like there's anything left to hide.'

'Hey, a man got to ask nowadays. Better to be safe than sorry, you know?'

'I know.'

'Cool. Text me your flight details and I'll have a cab ready to pick up you at the airport.'

'Okay. See you soon.'

I hung up and stared out the backseat window thinking about what I just agreed to. I started thinking about Viv. FUCK. I felt bad but then again, I don't know if I had any reason to. We never defined the thing we had. We didn't even know what we had. She told me I love you. But then again, those three words are just that. Words. People tell their pets I love you. Kids tell their teddy bears I love you. Artists tell their thousands and thousands of fans I love you. If I love you carried any weight in this world, we would all be arrested and jailed by the moral police. And yet I still felt bad. I didn't owe Viv much, but I knew I owed her *something*. A tiny fraction of my loyalty for the fraction of her heart I had taken. In this despicable world we all owe those who give us their time and attention a little bit of decency. That's the least we could do for someone that puts up with our shit. I didn't feel good as I pressed her number and waited for her to pick up.

'Hi Chuck. You okay?'

'I think so…'

'What's wrong? I know you and I know when something's up. I can hear it in your voice.'

'Okay look. There's this girl that's coming to Paris to spend the weekend at my apartment. I like you and I felt I owed you at least some sort of honesty.'

'Don't you know how that makes me feel?'

'I think I do.'

'Don't you know it hurts imagining you having sex with another woman?'

'I think I do.'

'So why are you doing it?'

'I don't know.'

She hung up.

She hadn't changed much as she paced around the room in my grey AC/DC tee with her underwear on. She had her blond curls tied in a bun, which for some unexplainable reason just put me off. Something was different. I don't know if it was her or me. But it was something.

'Why are you pacing around like that?'

She stopped and faced towards me. 'I don't know. I just feel restless. Let's do something!'

'Like what?'

'I don't care anything. Chuck I've been here since yesterday and the only thing we've done is eat, fuck and watched old movies.'

'That sounds like a great fucking day and a half to me.'

'That's because you're a boring old grinch.'

'FUUCKKK fine then. Get ready and let's go out for a walk.'

Being in Valeria's company wasn't bad but it wasn't enjoyable either. Sort of like how she was in bed. The first time we fucked when she arrived at my apartment, she possibly gave me the worst head I've ever received in my life as she went on her knees had her body between my legs and wrapped her mouth around my cock. Her spirit was in the right place, but her technique was off. Just a plain old bob and suck. Back and forth. See I was bougie and filthy when it came to oral sex. I gave the best and I wanted nothing but the best in return. A sloppy wet head was always appreciated. A man doesn't remember much about his past lovers, but he had a special place in his heart for the ones that gave great head. I looked down and pitied her as she gave it her all, working and slaving away like some factory worker. The second time I denied her advances to give me head. The third time I was awaken by her tongue circling around my cock as I laid there trying to my best to enjoy whatever she was attempting to accomplish. In the end I had to create a fantasy world in my mind just to maintain the erection. I daydreamed of me and Geneviève in a movie theatre watching my favorite romcom as she unbuckled by jeans pulled my cock out and started sucking. Her head moving up and down in a bouncing motion as those close to us and everybody else in the theatre switched their attention towards her.

'OH MY GOD LOOK AT THAT WHORE! SHE DOESN'T CARE IF ANYONE IS WATCHING!'

'SOMEONE PLEASE TELL THIS WOMAN THERE ARE TEENAGERS HERE TOO!!'

'LOOK PAUL LOOK HOW SHE'S SITTING ON TOP OF HIS COCK AND RIDING IT!! THAT GUY IS ONE LUCKY BASTARD I'LL TELL YOU THAT MUCH!!'

'TELL HER THAT I'M NEXT! I'M GOING TO STICK IT RIGHT UP HER ASS! I BETCHA I CAN FUCK HER BETTER THAN THAT UGLY SON OF A BITCH!!'

'LOOK AT HIS FACE HE'S NOT EVEN GOING TO LAST LONG!! OHH NOOO HE'S ABOUT TO CUM BEFORE HER! WHAT A SHAME. BABY GIRL YOU DESERVE MUCH BETTER THAN THIS LOUSY FUCK!! CALL ME.'

I drew Geneviève close to me thrusting harder and faster until I exploded all up in her vagina. Looking down watching my semen drip from her picturesquely created cunt and down her legs. I came back to reality opened my eyes and saw that Valeria had cum running down her mouth. She stared at me smiling.

'You liked that didn't you?'

'Yes, I did darling. You did great.'

The lies we tell to avoid the conversations our hearts can't bear to have.

I took her to the park where I met Jhené and we sat on the same bench where we first kissed. She put away her phone and looked at me.

'Why is your face always like that?'

'Like what?'

'You know…sad. You seem to have accomplished so much for someone your age and you've made a career out of doing something you love…and yet you still look miserable. Like life hasn't been good to you.'

'Everybody keep asking me why I'm sad and yet they all fail to realize that it's what I am. See most people try to shove their sadness away but I embraced mine. Because in a twisted way without that sadness I wouldn't be me. A girl I loved once told me that I live in a constant state of sadness. Which is true. Because truthfully that's the only place where I feel comfortable. Happiness isn't for me. Sadness is honest and genuine. Happiness is slimy and disguises itself wearing a mask with something bad behind it. Happiness is temporary and comes with several conditions. But sadness…Sadness doesn't require me to do or be anything.'

'Wow...interesting. I think I know why you're such a great writer now. Because every time you speak it sounds like you're writing a new page in a book. You write like a writer but unlike most authors you talk like one too.'

'Thank you. What about you? If I was to ask you why you are sad what would your answer be?'

'Hmm I don't know. As for me I'll lie and say I'm happy. It saves me the hassle of going in deep with it because I feel like no one truly cares. People don't really care or understand. Or they say just be happy or just do this. But I'm a hypocrite because I do take their advice and do shit. I think that's why I'm always busy and on the go. I don't like not being busy. It's more time to think. Hell, I even hate showering sometimes because it's time alone.'

'Hmm. That was a sad and beautiful answer. There might be a writer lurking deep in you Valeria.'

'The girl you said you loved once. What's her name?'

'Célia.'

'What happened?'

'She loved more, and I loved less. After a while the blindness caused by love faded away and she realized the mistake she had made. That night we shared in Strasbourg you mentioned that a broken heart can always spot its equal. Who broke yours?'

'A man that didn't appreciate what he had until it was no longer in his possession.'

'Did it hurt you?'

'I try to not think it did, but I would be lying if I said it didn't. But more so I think it just ruined love for me. I no longer know if I hate love or just despise men because the more men I meet the more those two become harder to separate.'

'I think we all hate love sometimes.'

'Do you think someone could ever have good love?'

'Once upon a time I did, but I no longer believe in good or bad love. Only *right* love. Love is subjective and we all have our own ideas and thoughts about it. You can be with the best person and they will still be the wrong lover for you. You can be in the most toxic relationship and you will still fight tooth and nail for it to work because no matter how complicated or difficult that person is, they are still the right one for you.'

'But how then do you know if you have something worth fighting for?'

'I honestly don't know. I thought I did.... But life proved me wrong.'

'Do you want to head back? I'm not restless anymore.'

'What do you want to do?'

'I don't care anything. As long as it includes me laying on the bed.'

'Okay. Let's go.'

We stood up and made our way back towards the apartment as I thought about the next imaginary place, I was going to fuck Geneviève.

The next day I walked her out to the cab that was taking her back to the airport standing there watching the car drive off until it was out of my sight before heading back into the apartment. I picked up my phone. It was 4.30pm. Viv would've been finished with her classes by now. I went on my recent calls and pressed on her number. Ring...ring...ring...ring...

'Hello.'

'Hi Viv, it's Chuck.'

'I know. I do have your number saved you know.'

'Okay. How are you? I miss yo-'

'Has that bitch left?'

'Yes.'

'Good. Did you fuck her?'

'Yes, I did. But I didn't enjoy it.'

'OHH FUCCK YOU CHUCK!! I honestly don't want to hear that bullshit. I already had a long and stressful day.'

'I'm being honest Viv. My soul is restless when it's taken away from your presence.'

'I don't know Chuck...I don't want this to be a repetitive thing and I certainly don't want to be one of the many women that fall for your tricks and charming words...I can't do this.'

'Please Viv. Please give me another chance. I'm never going to do this again and I will never put you in a situation like this again. I want you and in a weird way I need you. Being around you makes me feel nothing. And it's hard to find someone that makes you feel nothing in a world that forces us to feel something.

'Hmmm. I'll think about it.'

'There's no need to think. Come to mine this evening. I'll cook.'

'I'll think about it.'

'Please come. I miss you.'

'Okay...fine. When should I come?'

'Around 7.30.'

'Okay. That's fin-'

'Hold on Viv someone is calling me. I'll just see you later alright?'

'Okay.'

I accepted the other call.

'Hello?'

'Hi. Is this Charles Johnson?'

'Yes, I'm him. Who is this?'

'OH MY GOD NO WAY!! My name is Mona and I'm a literature student. I'm sorry for calling like this but I found your number online and I'm a big fan of your work. You're like my favorite author!'

'That's fine. Thank you, Mona.'

'Is it true that everything you write is based on your life?'

'Kind of.'

'Is it true that you've had sex with all the women you write about?'

'Yes.'

'Look I write poems too, and I live in Paris. Could I come over and show you my work?'

'I just write. I think what you're after is a publishing company.'

'I know. But could I come over and spend time with you? Please...'

'I can't tonight. I'm busy.'

'Okay. How about another day?'

'No. I'm busy then too.'

'I didn't even say which day it was.'

'It doesn't matter.'

'I'm 21 years old, beautiful and have curly hair.'

'That's good for you.'

'I would give you the best head you've ever had.'

'I bet you would.'

'So, can I come?'

'No.'

'PLEASEEEEE???'

'Goodbye Mona.'

I hung up and went to the bathroom to wash my face. I stared at my reflection in the mirror as I could feel the water dribble down my neck and onto my tee. I still looked like shit, but this time around I didn't feel like one.

The eyes have a way of showing what your soul feels and mine had a sprinkle of proudness in it on this humdrum day. I didn't precisely know what I felt but I knew it was something good. I put on my light blue denim jacket my red white and black Chicago Bulls trucker cap picked up my skateboard and walked out of the apartment as I told myself that death could *wait*

another day.

From the day you are born till the day you die you will

experience that this life can be one hell of a ride.

Hardships will come your way and you will have days

where you feel like you're *drowning*. On this somewhat

lonesome journey you can encounter pain that will take

a heavy toll on your heart and leave you crying. This

life is not easy, but you just have to keep your head up

and continue on your path without looking back.

Always set the bar high and never settle for anything

less than what you dream of but bear in mind that life

doesn't always go as planned so have a realistic eye.

You will experience a heartbreak or few but never stop

chasing *true* love and for those of you that have a

religious soul put your faith in the man above in

everything you do. Walk around with an open mind and

see how your knowledge will broaden with it. But most importantly never look down on someone and treat everybody with respect. Never let the pressures of this society ruin your happiness internally. When you come across good love, cherish and value it. Because when you have something good in life spend as much time you can with it and bask in the goodness of it before *reality* tries to take it away.

- *Charles Johnson*

Made in United States
Troutdale, OR
02/18/2025